THE BROKEN PANE
Not For Kids Vol. 1

Part 1

Jorge Harrington

i

Jorge Harrington

DEDICATION

Dedicated to Kristen Harrington

INTRODUCTION

This is my debut novel. The first part of a two part book, but the beginning of a series that the voices in my head, have drove me to write. I've always loved to read, and one day I wanted to write my first book.

No matter how long or short, hard or easy, or good or bad, I wanted to reach my goal and do what I'm passionate about. My mentors and role models for my dream, would be the two kings in writing. The king of horror: Stephen King, and the king of hearts: Nicholas Sparks. Having these two authors in the world, has inspired me to write my heart out.

I originally came up with the idea to do a story about a witch in the modern times, while driving on a road. I thought while driving home one day, *What if a witch really existed today? What would she accomplish here in a small town? How would she get her powers?*

All these thoughts started to form the character October Blue, an old woman that has given nothing but good to the world, and in return she couldn't do what she wanted in life, and that was to have a child.

Being taught in English class in 6th grade, that it wasn't the blood and gore that made horror, but it was the things that go bump in the night, wondering what made that sound in the first place. Blood and gore would be a cherry on top of a tasty cake, but it was never to actually be the whole reason behind horror.

The more I thought of my characters, the more I fell in love with them. Making it harder for me to do the things I've done in this first part. That was scary in itself, But it was a joy to see how the story unfolded, because in reality; the story wrote itself. I found that hard to believe at first, but its true. Any other writer would agree with me.

Part 2 of The Broken Pane is writing itself at the moment. The story is coming in like a television series, where it builds to a climax that leaves you feeling fulfilled. The first part would be dinner and the second would be the desert.

I really hope you enjoy the story. Even though it is a figment of my Imagination, it felt real as every word hit my computer screen. Enjoy Reader.

Sincerely,

Jorge Harrington

ACKNOWLEDGMENTS

This story wouldn't be what it is today, without the influences from my family and friends. My wife Kristen, who just so happened to have a soft spot for nerds, found me and gave me three wonderful sons. Also having a foreign exchange student named Linda, has fit perfectly into our family.

My friends, Daniel, Ryan, Nick, Gerald, Ethan, Tristin, Darren, Matt, Lacy, Jay, RJ Smith, Curtis, Amanda, and so much more. Believe me, there is so many of you guys. It was you guys that formed me into the guy I am today. If I were to thank every single one of you individually, this Acknowledgment would be a book in itself.

I would also like to thank Caelin for helping me bring this first part together. I hope she will help me again with part 2 of The Broken Pane, and possibly on more books in the Not For Kids Series.

THE BROKEN PANE
Not For Kids Vol 1

Part 1

Jorge Harrington

CHAPTER 1

HER NAME WAS OCTOBER Blu, sitting on her porch, in the mid-afternoon of June. The heat was on its way. It would be almost August before it became a scorcher. She was a stay at home wife that cleaned house, prepared meals, and kept up the yard. She and her husband, Rake, were well off.

Rake never liked to show off the money he made from plowing the fields, so it was yard sales and thrift stores, with the help of a few coupons. The Blus had a ton of spending money after bills. It was the aroma of clean that made Mrs. Blu smile. A clean house-equaled a clean life; especially when you had the money for the bleach to get the job done.

Another smell was escaping out of the open window, on the north side of the house. Something that she did made habit of , no matter the weather or the purpose. This always put October in a grand mood. The pie's smell, and the smell of a ham in the oven, mad the whole farm hungry. Cooking was one of October's favorite things to do, like an artist loved to paint, she would make a work of art almost every day.

When her husband would call it quits for the day, dinner would be ready to be served. It wasn't just a plain piece of meat sitting in a hot oven, no, fresh pineapple was dangling of it with a glaze that would make a master chef jealous. Baked potatoes with a cream cheese and fresh bacon-bits were ready to be sprinkled on top. Rake loved Parmesan on his, October made sure she got the latest date at Big Shop before buying it. Mixed vegetables for sides, with the right combination of spices, that would make any husband proud to have a wife like her.

She was rocking back and forth in her chair, with her nose buried in a book. Crack to a drug addict, October loved to read. There was no chance in hell, that she would get diagnosed with Alzheimer, because she had been reading since she learned her ABC's, it almost felt like. Rake didn't care too much for it; he left all the reading up to her when they filled out taxes and important letters.

The book she was reading was written by one of her favorite Authors of all time, Stephen King. She had been reading him ever since she discovered his novel: Carrie, sitting on a book rack at the Plymouth gas station, just before you entered into Victoria, Oregon. Dr. Sleep was the title, and Mr. King's picture took up the whole back of the cover, with eyes for days. He sure knew how to woo a woman, his writing mad e October have fantasies of kissing and other unmentionable tasks, that the human body could do with. Her book mark was five pages away from the ending, and she was loving it. She was going to savor the ending for the next morning, that way boredom wouldn't creep up on her and catch her off guard.

She was 56 years old, the same age as Stephen King. That made her love him more and more; every time she thought about it. She was practically growing up alongside him. Rake was her heart throughout the years, but she would most defiantly would have chosen Stephen if ever there was a rare choice in the matter.

But Rake was the one that pulled her heart strings, and would be married for thirty-one years in February, an accomplishment that only few would be proud of in this time and age. Plymouth was well known for its underage pregnancies and single parent families.

October wished that she had some little ones to chase around, but due to a defect in her uterus, she was unable, and the tries and prayers were never answered. Instead, they adopted two black labs as pups named Bruno and Einstein that filled the void of children a tad, but not the full. They would run free through the corn fields and cabbage patches, that made up most of Plymouth, and would never so much as go as far as the road leading into the town Victoria. Occasionally they would ride with Rake in the blue truck to help keep him company, when he would spray for weeds on the four wheeler. Not today though, today's job was to set up pipe in field number 7, which was to produce cabbage. The only cabbage patch this year.

Plymouth was quiet, only noise it made when you listened really close was the engine of a tractor that Rake was driving, or down town where it only consisted of gas stations, barber shops, and knick knack shops that made a small strip-if you blinked you would miss it. But, sometimes the silence got to October, and the loneliness sunk in, making her read more and more. The book made her escape this curse of waiting at home for her lovely to come home, day in and day out. She hadn't any friends, not by choice, but that was what life carved for her future. She had Rake and her pups, but she didn't have any other beacon of communication. A cell phone only for calls to her husband, and to the stores that she shopped at, in order to save an extra penny. She was great at that.

Rake would put bread on the table-literally-and she would do her best to spend as little as she possibly could on the want items, then the needed items.

Rake however was the one with the friends. She was kind to them, but she never took the time to invite them over for coffee, or a movie night, or even allowed herself to be invited to. He was friends with the Figgs that were sort of neighbors to her, but to Rake, they were friends that have been grandfathered into her life on his accord. They lived six corn fields to the north of the Blu farm, which was nice for her husband when he decided to visit on his breaks, he could.

Not for a few years now, he didn't.

A tragedy had fallen upon the Figgs family. One that set the first law to ever hinder texting and driving in all fifty states. They became celebrities in that way, not a fame that was proud of or congratulated, but one that had broken and warped the family for the rest of their lives. Richard Figgs was the father, and is the father of his four daughters: Ruth, (the oldest, age twenty -five) Rachael, (sixteen) and the twins, Barbara and Ella. The death of their mother, Bethany, was all over the news and the front cover of the Now Newspaper for a long month.

They were just neighbors now, ones that minded their own business.

October put her book mark in her spot and got out of her rocking chair and made her way into her home. The clock above the love seat read, six o' clock sharp, Rake would be calling it a day now, maybe even parking the John Deere he liked to call the Grinch right this moment, and would be making his way back shortly. She would have the table set, and the food prepared and ready for eating before he even kicked off his boot.

The ham was perfect. She sliced the four round pieces with the electric knife, and stacked them neatly next to the vegetables and taters, covering the whole plate with good grub. October placed her plate in the microwave and his in the oven, wouldn't be too long now, she even stole a few bites of the pineapple while she waited. She always ate with her husband, like a good wife should. There were two beers in the freezer that she put in, so they were their coldest when Rake decided to have one.

He always did.

CHAPTER 2

THE FARMER HAD PARKED his truck at the end of the gravel drive way, almost a kiss away from the silver Honda that his wife owned. He was six foot two, with a long full beard that had gotten some gray in it at the tip, close to the top of his Pecs. Farming was a workout that he knew well, and did in routine every year. He was a gentle giant that would try his best to give the world to October if his abilities would allow him to.

The frame of him was built like a tree, and his definition was very obvious, for a sixty-one year old man. He had to duck every time he went into the house, like he did right now, after he had been welcomed with licks and barks from Bruno and Einstein. They too were like family that he always seemed to baby whenever he had the chance. He always made a habit of reminding his wife to feed and water them, every morning, with a note that hung on the fridge.

Rake kicked off his boots before stepping onto the carpet, and hung his hat on the coat rack to the left of him. When those pieces of clothing were removed, it was a symbolism of relaxation that the farmer always looked forward to ritually.

"Damn October, that sure smells good. I seem to come home at the right time, every time, to get it while it's fresh." Rake reached into the freezer and pulled out the two frosted brews, and popped one open, upon sitting down at the table. "I'm

Starving Marvin love. What have you cooked up tonight?"

"What does it smell like?" She rested her hand on the stove's handle, like a show girl, waiting to reveal the shiny new car behind the curtain. "No, it's not spaghetti. You always say that when I make you guess."

"Fair enough. I guess I smell potatoes, so did you make breakfast for dinner?"

"You love breakfast foods, almost as much as the sun loves to shine." October opened the door and pulled out the plate of food for her husband. "I made us baked taters, with ham and vegetables. You got the potatoes right . . . sort of." She set the plate in front of him, then retrieved hers and sat across from her partner. October always loved it when he was home. He was cute when he played along with her guessing games.

Before the couple engaged in eating their supper, Rake planted a kiss on his wife's lips, to show that he had missed her while she was out. He didn't understand how she can just wait on him while he was out for long hours at a time. They didn't have texting, only made phone calls to one another, when there were only important things to say. Both had reached that limit of finding out new things about each other. Now they just talked about each other's day, one that only consisted of him telling her he had worked on a field, and she had read another book.

"So how was your day love?" Rake didn't like the silence very much. He spent most of his time working in silence that he had to engage into any kind of conversation. Even if it meant a re-run of last night. "Did you make sure the dogs had their fixens?"

"Of course I did Rake. You never let me forget since the day they were pups." October took two bites of her potato, before she drank from her glass of orange juice. "It is part of my routine when I clean. Now, don't get all "I shouldn't write another note tomorrow. By all means, it's what I look forward to every day when I make breakfast for myself in the morning. You do your job, and I'll do mine".

"Well you know me too well, honey. I just sometimes get this strong fear, that they're going to kill over one day, and that I'm just going to lose it."

"I sure do hope something like that doesn't happen at all. We should set a goal, to live forever". October joked. She took another drink, and killed her vegetables.

Rake laughed at this. "That would be nice, but if something like that would happen, it would naturally be creepy to me."

"Why?"

"Because all humans die and we try to stop the inevitable, but we're always going to die by accident or natural, no matter how long we go to the doctor. If I go, I wanna go while I dream in my bed." The farmer had finished his brew and all of his ham, while he watched his wife pour another glass for herself. But, just behind her, he saw the large spine of Dr. Sleep, resting on the counter near the sink.

"That book is going to distract you from me." Said Rake, a piece of pineapple was stuck in his teeth, making him look like he was sixteen again. He knew that when his wife was reading and that she wanted to talk about it to him, even though she knew that he didn't care for it. But this time, he wanted to be the good guy and ask about it first, so there wouldn't be any awkward tension between them, when she did. "What page you on, anyway?"

"Almost done with it. I'm so close to the end. I thought I would savor the last few pages for tomorrow, before I went into Victoria, to get some things from Big Shop." October thought he would never ask her. "Haven't decided though. What do you think I should do?"

"I really don't care babe. I was just wondering, you speed through those damn things pretty fast. I can't tell what story you're telling me, or anything."

His wife's passion for reading was so great, she could have two, almost three books read in a week. That was twelve novels a month, a number that was too large for him to comprehend, when you added up thirty-one years of marriage. Her reading meant that he wasn't getting any pune. Something that had been happening for at least twenty-years. Yes, their attempts to have children were failures and often. But, since they learned to cope-he did anyways-with it, that they would be making love like jack rabbits. Or teens that didn't have any boundaries or fears of some parents finding out, or that their daughter was sneaking behind their backs.

But, in Rake's case, he was a married loner.

"I love that you love to read. You always seem so happy when I get home." He lied through his teeth, but his October didn't pick up a trace of it.

"Thanks hun. I am happy when I do. I get even happier when your home, and notice that I'm glowing. Are you done love? I am." October rose up and put her plate in the sink and rinsed it. She came to retrieve Rake's with her hand out, waiting for his response.

"Yes I am. Just gonna down the rest of my potato, skin and all." He chuckled, and let her take the plate. While he licked the butter, that formed around his lips. "Thanks honey, it was delicious as always."

CHAPTER 3

THERE WERE TWO BATHROOMS in the Blu's house. One in the master bedroom at the end of the hallway, and the other one at the beginning. Two spare rooms on the left side, and a laundry room and a closet were on the right. The far bathroom had no lock on it, but the other one did. For reasons unknown, that was how the house was made.

While October cleaned the little dishes that were dirty from tonight's supper. Rake needed to relieve himself - number two - and kindly told his wife that he needed to use the little boy's room. She waved him off with a 'whatever attitude', and continued to her cleaning. He never used the master's water closet after dinner, for the secret ritual that he was performing, to make up for all those lost years.

He had already started, by telling October of his private business, to buy himself a solid fifteen minutes. Then he quietly turn the lock on the doorknob, so she wouldn't hear the clicking sound it made, in order to keep her from asking further questions of his intentions. Even though, what he did was none of her business, unless he wanted her to know. He would get nervous, that she had the ability to see through walls, catching him in the act.

The mirror above the marble sink was a large one. His reflection welcomed him, and wondered if he really needed to use this place, for its proper use or if he was going to use it for his own personal gain. Rake knew the answer to his own question of course, giving himself a sly wink, before opening up the cupboard doors beneath the sink.

There he found cleaning supplies of Mr. Erryware cleaning spray, along with extra towels, toilet paper, and scrub sponges. But, that wasn't his goal. It was what was taped to the back of the sink that he wanted. He again, slowly peeled the pictures of the cold surface, to silence the sound of paper being rustled in his hand.

Only three minutes went by, but it seemed that he out did his welcome by the time he pulled his drawers down, and sat on the porcelain throne. He gave a fake cough, so he could locate the whereabouts of the female partner in the kitchen. He heard a faint clink of some sort, and the rushing of well water, that fell over the dirty plates and into the drain below. *Good*, he thought. Then continued his bad habit, that he let consume him all these years.

Four palm size photos rested on his knee, while he looked at them one at a time, with great pleasure and a high sense of desire. They were pictures of four naked eighteen year old girls that were doing the deed with some lucky gent, with their hair and make-up all in a beautiful mess. One cheerleader, wanted to be the cheer squad leader so bad, that she had to get on her knees and beg for it.

Another one was of a student that was in dire need to be taught a lesson on bad dress code. Wearing a skirt with no panties and see through dress shirt was enough to get her sent to the principle office, and would have to beat erasers.

They were like golden cheese to the hungry mouse's eyes. Rake loved them and often thought about them, almost every single day. His hand went to his skin flute, and was doing October's job, but had neglected it and him all together. He didn't need her when he had his four paper girlfriends, just waiting for him to have a happy ending, here and there.

Rake often thought that he wasn't trying hard enough, and that he had to spice her up with romance. But hit a brick wall, when she pulled away or told him what he didn't want to hear, every single time. She would pick her stupid books over him - telling him that she couldn't put her book down, and that she was too side track to even begin to make love right now.

"You didn't fall in did you?" Came the wife's voice, she must have done her cleaning for the day finally. It caught Rake off guard that he stopped right before his climax so she wouldn't hear his heavy breathing. "I was going to remind you that the pipe is leaking in there, so you better wash your hands in the back bathroom, or here in the kitchen, so there isn't a huge mess."

"Good to know." Rake answered. His hard on had gone away, leaving him with blue balls, blue balls like his damn name. He didn't like to be disturbed when he was beating off to the queens of hearts, the ones that always seem to help him be truly relaxed.

He finished his business, and pulled up his jeans, the look of disappointment was clear on his face. The tune of humming was escaping his lips, so he could be in a better mood when he faced his wife. She will notice his expressions, so he wanted her to think that everything was alright in his world, she always noticed and always asked.

Back under the sink they went with such ease. October would never know they were under there, because she always uses the bedroom's toilet, and hadn't found them out in so long. Rake admitted to himself that he didn't have a back bone, when it came to taking control, and giving it to his wife. *Maybe tonight she'll be in the mood? There is only one way to find out sir, but then again she always shot you down. If she did, it wouldn't make a difference, you'll still be looking at those nasty pictures.* He was right. Tonight he would try, and if she didn't want to, he wouldn't be bothered by it. With inspiring thoughts, Rake went out to wash his hands in the kitchen.

CHAPTER 4

WHILE RAKE TOOK HIS shower in the other room, October finally came to the conclusion that she would finish Dr. Sleep in the morning, before she went to Big Shop to get some needed things like milk, spare ribs for tomorrow's supper, cooking oil, and some more spices. She wrote her grocery list on the table, then setting it under her book, so when she was ready to leave, there it would be for her to take.

The Blu's always went to bed early and always got up before the sun. Even though Rake didn't really need to start farming until eight, he still would get up an hour early to drink a whole pot of coffee, before he headed out the door. Rake will get out of the shower, then spend most of his time brushing out his beard - so it would be smooth when he got out of bed, and that way when he ran his fingers through it, they wouldn't get caught in a snag, hurting his face - finally, he would crawl into bed and fall fast asleep.

As October finished her list, making sure she hadn't forgotten anything. She caught herself thinking about kids, and her list, and why it was so small. Damn uterus, messed up everything in her life. A three bedroom house with no kids to sleep in, a fridge that was filled so two people can survive off. Not to mention, she hadn't blown Rake off in quite some time, nor even been touched by him inappropriately. Ever since they discovered they couldn't conceive a baby - in the five years that they tried - October had been everything, but in the mood. Why try to make a baby, when the results weren't like normal people. They could adopt. But she declined, knowing if it wasn't meant to be, then she wouldn't want someone else's baby. It was all her fault her husband wasn't sexually active towards her and she wondered why he had even stayed with her.

The voice of her mother entered her head, like a devil wearing a halo for a crown. *My poor baby, I told you if you were sneaking behind old mamma's back, you would be cursed with something. Don't say I didn't warn you.* He mother was right. She had been banging no-no parts with boys since she was sixteen, jumping on the band wagon with all the other females in this area. No one ever waited till they were married anymore, that was *so last years in.* October's mother died of AIDS, shortly after that comment. She later was put in the care of her father, making her move up to Plymouth, who later committed suicide, one random right.

She met Rake shortly after high school. He had swept her off her feet, and she fell fast and hard for him. He was quite the jokester and a hard worker, owning a few pieces of land, at the age of twenty-one.

Somewhere in her crazy life she lost the drive to give her husband pleasure. Some where she had given up on a slice of human naturalism, and there was no turning back now.

When she was done with getting her things situated, like double checking the stove to make sure that it was off, checking to see if all the doors were dead bolted; that sort of thing. She walked down to her bedroom and laid herself next to her husband. Who like she predicted was sound asleep, and had the covers pulled all the way up to his hairy chin. He hadn't even bothered to say good night or give a kiss, let alone on the cheek. She still liked those things.

But sleep was coming; she brushed her tad disappointment off her shoulder, and did the same as Rake. Ready to be taken on the magical ferry on its way to Dreamland. This time thought, the destination was canceled, and was on its way to a nightmare that would change the life of Mrs. Blu entirely.

Jorge Harrington

- - - - -

The day was bright and calm. October was having herself a cup of coffee, with hazelnut cream swirling around in her drink. She was alone. The day was beaming down onto her hard, as she enjoyed herself in the middle of an enchanting park, at a picnic table. A view of two very large hills, and a town was formed in the middle, made up of brown and yellow buildings from where she could see. They looked like oversize boxes of Cheerios, stacked on top of one another.

She sat there without a care in the world. She didn't know why, she didn't know where. But, she did know that the quiet was soothing . . . for now. She was used to it, all those days being lonely in the house, with only messes to clean up and dogs to keep feeding. Now, she felt out of place, and wanted to go back home. Maybe because it was too quiet. The worry though, found a way to creep into the mind of October, and set her on edge. Who was going to clean those messes? Who was going to prepare food, when the two legged and the four legged was hungry?

The Broken Pane

Her hair was down. Brunette strands of hair flowed over her night gown that she suddenly realized that she was wearing, for all the public to see, wherever this park was stationed at. Out of place, like going to school in your underwear - or in the adult world - being seen by other adults as they went about their business, to just stop and stare and point. But they wouldn't get that chance, because it began to pour rain, hard and fast, after a thunder struck that had made the old farmer's wife jump out of her seating.

*She held herself, wondering what to do. **My god**, she thought as the world seemed foreign to her and this was the first time she had discovered it. Behind her was a group of trees that blocked off her exit, the back door to a wet situation. As she hoped that there would be some way out that way, there was none. Nothing but the arms of lively nature, that held hands like the Red Rover game, waiting for her to try to come over.*

The wind had picked up, making her gown swim to the left and tightening around her breasts and bum, causing a see through effect.

She really wasn't wearing underwear, only a wet rag it that danced in the rain.

Glancing back towards the projects of yellow and brown; that was her mission now. It was only before she went to take the first step towards a safe haven - if it was one - that she noticed our of her peripheral vision, that a dark figure had emerged out of the hand holding game, that the trees were playing. A large man, resembling Paul Bunyan, with his body and beard tattooed in black. His eyes though, were white like two flashlights side by side, eyeing that scared maiden with cruel intentions. Did he want to hurt her? You never talk to strangers, especially ones that look like hungry psychos that had its eye on some fresh meat.

He had only taken one step forward, but it was enough to get October sprinting towards the hills. Her hands were like arrows, out in front of her so she didn't somehow stray away from the task at hand. The grass felt like a titanic sponge, absorbing the drops of water and her steps, making her feel like she was running on a treadmill. She was covering good ground;

the projects were coming in clearly as she approached upon it fast.

"Hey!" A voice sounded like it has smoked a carton of cigarettes, every day that it had been in this world. It caught her off guard, making her cry out like she had been poked in the eye with a needle. Her destination never seemed so close, only far and out of reach. It was hard to tell that she was crying with all the rain, but they were there plain as the darkness that spoke behind her.

Boom! Boom! Boom! Yelled her heart, as it tried to escape her rib cage. The blood was sent throughout her body, that the pounding was inside her head now, causing it to dip forward with the uncontrollable weight. "Hey there little gir! Where you going? Why the hurry? Let me take you by the hand little gir!"

Hairy hands formed on top of October's shoulders. Making her jump in fear, and she would have fallen, but the claws had their grip on her like the cork in the wine bottle. Oh how she wanted to wake up. This wasn't real, she knew that, but all that shit about making the dream your own was nothing more than a myth. A lie, told over and over again, until it sounded like the truth.

"Don't worry I got you gir. I haven't seen a fair maiden like you round these parts . . . finally!" The lumberjack had put his lips on her ear, and stole a kiss. "Those aren't a place to be safe, no gir! I'll take you to a place where the honey is much, and the service is often!"

She was being lifted off the ground, like vultures pick up the tiny animals for food. The screams were horrifying. They pierced the black and blue sky, like the harpoon does in the back of the sperm whale, spilling blood and curdling it. When you die, you're supposed to wake up. But that could be a lie too. October was disappearing with the dark bearded man into the sky, watching the buildings minimize into nothing. Still hurling the word "no" down at them. No one was listening.

CHAPTER 5

RAKE WAS SLEEPING WITH a smile on his face. The choice to put the moves on his beautiful wife was tempting; he refrained from his urges, in order to not be shut down for doing the male normality. He was asleep before October, while she checked all the doors and made sure she skimmed the living quarters for new dust, something that she did well and often. He wanted to be asleep before she went to bed, because he had grown tired of being the little dogie that followed behind, hoping to get some pussy that never was available.

He had only been asleep for about two hours, before the moaning and the constant moving, was happening behind him. He ignored it a first, only opening his eyes for a moment to see her having her dream, then fell back to sleep. It was only for a second, when she had sat up, like the boogeyman did in that Halloween movie, screaming so loud. She was on the verge of busting her voice box, it sounded like. Her hair was a waded mess of sweat and saliva, as was her gown, making the room smell distasteful.

October's sudden sit-up made Rake fall out of bed in the means to duck and cover. His end-table was knocked over by the fall. Had it been a few inches closer to the end of the bed, Rake would have landed on it, and it would have collapsed under the weight of a large farmer.

Half asleep, felt like he was in a drunken stupor, trying to recollect and stand up was more than a chore.

When he did stand, he found the scene of his wife clawing at the nothing in the room. He stood, and made his way over to her side of the bed, in order to try to exercise her back to herself. He was there for his wife, like a good husband does, but sometimes a man doesn't know what to do.

"Tober! Honey! You're having a bad dream." He placed his hands on her shoulders in order to calm whatever demon had possessed her. She felt like she was made of stone. Rake was impressed with the strength of his wife, because she hadn't picked up anything heavier than a broom in her whole life. "Baby! Wake up!"

October's eyes were open, but they weren't seeing, they were just windows to a house with all the lights off. He didn't know what to do. If he did he would have done it. He did read an article in the paper, about how to send a jolt through someone, in order to snap them out of a tantrum or a fit; this was sort of on the lines of that. But nonetheless, he gave it a try and struck his wife across the face, fast and firm to find out.

It did the trick, in the sense of knocking her back into her pillow and shutting her up. She just lay there for a couple of seconds, not moving and breathing normally, like it had never happened. He would have to do some explaining of why he had laid the back of his hand on her cheek, once she woke.

She stirred a little, only a little. Rake thought he had given her a heart attack from his little quirk, but she looked fine by him. That was when he felt the bed become warm, then wet, and his ass was soaked by the time he realized, she had pissed the bed. It was a surprise to him deeply, because he stopped wetting the bed when he was seven.

His wife was having a nightmare that seemed to be the puppet master, and he had severed the strings and this was the outcome. It was the damn book that did this too her. He knew that reading was bad from the start; it had made her mess herself and trapped her in a prison of bad thoughts and possession. He wanted to be a good husband and save her from her obsession, she wasn't supposed to be like this.

Dreams are the last thought before you fall under the sandman's spell, thoughts that didn't have him in them. They never had him in them, if she would just make love to him once in a fucking blue moon, this would never have happened. Rake truly believed this, and this was the last straw.

"Tober! Tober! Wake up!" The urine ran down his leg, as he stood up and used his voice as a weapon.

October's eyes had come open fast. She looked around in the dark and saw that Rake was no longer to her left, but at her right, stomping towards the switch on the wall. When the light came, she was blinded by its brightness and closed her eyes as hard as she had opened them.

"Honey? What's going on?" She asked, more alert than a few seconds ago.

"You've just pissed the bed sweetie. It's all over me now, and you're sitting in it like you're part of its soup." Rake's leg hairs were glistening in the light's gleam.

"Oh my god! I . . . I'm sorry. I don't know what to say. I'm so embarrassed."

"Well this is disgusting. I can't say anything either, but I can do something about it. It's that damn book you've been reading Tober. I knew that sitting at home reading all the time was a bad thing, you've become sick over all of it, and I'm going to cure it." Rake opened the bedroom door, and stormed down the hallway.

"Rake! Where are you going?" October swung her legs out to the side of the bed. But they caught in the wet blank, that was more like a rag thickly damped in the yellow water, causing her to take a header onto the floor.

The sudden thud, made Rake stop in his tracks and look back towards the noise. It was a concerning sound, but old farmer thought it would be better to finish his mission on the cure for his wife. He hated himself for not checking, but he knew that this would continue if he gave in once again to his wife's obsession to read.

The lights traveled with Rake as he was turning them on as he finished his journey to the kitchen to where he had last seen his wife making out a grocery list before he had his nightly wash in the tub. Clean, just like she liked it. It made searching easier, that he did thank October for.

There was footsteps getting louder now, whatever that thud was, she must have recovered from it. Now, it was a matter of seconds before the fireworks went off, and the first fight in ten years was going to begin. This he knew. A male always seems to know when he has upset his spouse, and was going to pay in some way or another.

"What the fuck are you walking away from me?" yelled October. She had caught up with him finally and tried to pull on his shoulder. But the large bearded tank had yanked his arm free from her hard and fast. "It was an accident! Just a bad dream you stupid fucking man! I thought you would be caring and help me!'

"Oh I'm helping you alright Tober! It's that damn book that you read, it's filled your head full of demons and you can't shake them off. I don't want no evil in this house!" Rake had spotted it resting on the kitchen counter along with the list of things to get. He looked almost excited to see it, and like the basketball player dunks the ball in the hoop, Rake had done the something and tore the book from the counter. "Respect me!"

"No!" October pleaded with her love. She had come to tears and was reaching for the book that she had yet to finish. "Leave it be! It's mine; I'll do something with it. Just put the

The Broken Pane

The arguing and the pleading had awakened Bruno and Einstein from the horse trailer, where they slept their nights, waiting for the master to bring food and to give them love. They too were pleading with their barks which broke the night's silence like the sound of a glass break. They weren't tied up - the female master had forgotten to do that before she went to her place of sleep - so they made their way to the sliding door that was the back of the kitchen and the dining room.

The dog's barks if translated would have sounded like, "What's going on! What's going on! Let me in! Let me in!" The two pups were worried for their masters, but would somehow protect them from each other, if that big see through force field would move out of the way, like the male master does. They both frantically scratched at the glass, and whined in between each other's barks.

"This is evil Tober. You didn't see what I have seen in that room. My mind can't grasp the thought of what could have been doing that to you. You looked like the exorcist."

"Well I'm fine now and covered in piss, so if you don't mind handing me the book and helping me clean the sheets, so we can go back to bed." His wife's hand was out stretched in front of her like a baby would reach for the cookie jar on the tall table.

"No I won't. These books are never to be in my house again." Rake gave her a firm look, like the looks her mother gave her when she was misbehaving, and was caught doing it. Then her husband started tearing the book in front of her. Ripping out the pages, and murdering Dr. Sleep beyond recognition. He even grabbed the knife scissors from the knife block, and was cutting the pages into little bits so she couldn't put them back together when he decided he was done killing.

"I hate you! You're a fucking joke of a man. I'll never forgive you for what you've done. When you're done, you get the hell out of this house. SHUT THE FUCK UP

DOGS!" October searched for something to throw. When she found a marble bowl on the living room coffee table, she had chucked it, along with all the contents inside it, at the sliding glass door, shattering it instantly. It was intended for the forehead of the man she called her husband, but now called a bastard and stupid, but lashing out in anger always clouds some form of judgment.

"Don't you throw shit at my dogs!" Rake too had wanted to throw something too. Because before she knew it, she had ducked out of the way, and heard what was left of her book crash against the wall behind her.

"Get out! Get out! Don't touch me!" screamed the farmer's wife. Bruno and Einstein had finally made it in the house, after running away from that feeding dish that flew like a Frisbee at them. They both were barking at the male master, with a look on their face that was very convincing. It was time for Rake to get out.

The word 'Sorry' was on his lips. But he made the choice to use it for another time, a time that was later, rather than sooner. There wasn't another word spoken, screamed, or barked, while she waited for Rake to change and get some clothes for his morning. Her and her two pups stayed in the kitchen and waited. October's arms were crossed, and she tried to weep silently as much as possible.

Finally the man emerged from the hall, and walked passed his family without even a glance out the door, with a giant slam. That was when October let the tears flow and she dropped to her knees. The paper bits stuck to her like flies to the sticky paper. Dr. Sleep was gone now, and all over a stupid night terror.

Bruno had walked over to the front door and marked his territory, before joining his brother in giving October licks on the cheek, to help ease the pain. It worked, but very little.

CHAPTER 6

A HOT AFTERNOON DAY had consumed the town of Victoria, and was cooking all the cars that sat in the Big Shop's parking lot. One giant parking lot that was able to hold a quarter of the town's population, and was a mean bitch to get out of once you're in.

The economy was still in recovery from its black days, so the state of Oregon decided to make Big Shops in every county, in order to have all customers fund all their money into one big piggy bank. The whole foundation was owned by a bank that made up a majority of the marketplace. The rest was a grocery store that had thirty lanes, that were up and running twenty four hours of the day, with a repair tech at arm's reach in case of a faulty check stand. Twenty-five loading docks, five on each side of the building except the north of it had seven. It had four floors of money sucking businesses, which sold to the needy and the wants.

Sometimes it was often referred to as the butt-hole of Victoria, and us pee-ons were all heading towards it with all kinds of endeavors. A huge inside joke, that everyone was in on. The rest of the town was made up of houses, a hospital, and gas stations that were very well spread out evenly throughout the neighborhoods. That part of the town was called 'the body', a much defined body, that didn't get enough attention as the butt-hole did.

The grocery part was what October was most interested in. She had cleaned up the mess the next morning, also taping up the broken sliding door with cardboard and duct tape, then grabbed the list - which was also damaged in the strapping of the book - and went shopping anyways. The house never seemed so haunted after the outburst, making October feel like she needed to escape from its gray feeling.

Only a few items was what she needed to get, but when she got them, that meant she had to go back home. She wasn't ready. So pushing the cart around the store and watching all the other problems and solutions in the world, live out in front of her, was a tad soothing.

Some child had snuck a candy bar into his pocket, only to have his dad find him doing it, and then threaten him with discipline right in front of everyone. An old man was being pushed around in his wheel chair by his daughter, trying to make him get out of the hospital for a little bit it seemed. The poor guy looked like death, and the girl had stress lines around her eyes from the constant crying. Another child was back talking his mother, so when no one was looking, she had popped the little boy in the mouth, then continued shopping over his cries. She didn't care. Nobody else seemed to either.

October had walked miles around and around, contemplating her return, contemplating Dr. Sleep and his ending. Maybe they had another copy on the second floor? She doubted it, because it was on the best-sellers list for its third week now, and the chances were slim to none. But maybe someone had left one lying around, or there was one left that no one had bought yet.

The elevator was the fastest way to get around in this clown house. Each lift could hold thirty people at a time, and there was no carts allowed in them. So the book loving farmer's wife, purchased her items and stood in the lift with ten or so average Janes and Joes. A two minute ride to the general merchandise of the business, a very popular part of the store, considering it was filled with clothes and electronics. It was the books in the very back that was of more interest to October.

The shelves had a shiny finish on them, giving the books an even more inviting look. October could have easily given up on the book right then and there, but she couldn't stand the thought that she was right there at the end. It almost broke her heart just thinking about the last few pages in the book. Moving on was like, getting rid of the pain in her cheek in mere seconds, couldn't be done and time only heals all wounds.

Big Shop had a tremendous amount of selection on literature, especially on young teens. But October longed for the king of horror, and the new releases section was bare, just like she feared it would be. She stood and looked at the bookshelf, like she was trying to win a staring contest with it. How long did she have to wait till people would stop buying it? How long did she have to wait till she was welcomed into the readers loop?

"That darn book isn't coming back for a couple months. It's all over the news". Said a voice, causing October to lose her battle with the wooden shelf. "It's been all over the news . . . well the news on reading anyways."

October turned her attention to the owner of the voice. A tween girl that looked like she had barely grown into a B cup size, and had the blackest hair she had ever seen, that the light reflected off of the surface. She was a little dirty, with no makeup, and was skinny that her shirt looked like a mini tent-just hung of her like she didn't care about her appearance.

"Thank you." Answered October. "I just really would like a copy, and I was so sure that there would have been at least one book sitting on the shelf. I did have a copy, but now I don't."

"What happened?"

"I don't want to talk about it. What did you say your name was?"

"I didn't. You can call me Sophia . . . and sorry that I surprised you. I've always been taught never to talk to strangers;

something that I never seem to get through my thick skull. You just looked so sad, thought I would give you a little heads up is all."

October looked her up and down, thinking about the turn of events that lead her to a girl that talked to strangers. She should be in school, or be along with her mother in the clothes department. It was off setting and out of the ordinary. Then again, October never knew how kids acted this day and time-shocked even-this girl didn't look like she was pregnant like the other percent of females.

"How old are you?"

"Twelve."

"Your mother just lets you wander around on your own like this?"

"My parents are dead."

A change of the subject made October bend over and look Sophia in her bright green eyes. "I am so sorry. I don't get out much and socialize with people as often as

I like to. I didn't know." Her voice was sympathetic.

"It's fine. They died when I was like three or four, I wouldn't be able to remember them even if I tried. No pictures either. You don't have to be sorry; I would have the same happiness if they *were* here like I do now." Sophia leaned in and stole a hug to the woman, holding the bags of groceries in her hand. October didn't move. She let the girl hug her, but was surprised again, like a scientist discovering a new species. Strange children also hugged strangers, it was unheard of.

"By the way, I know a place that might have the book you are looking for."

"You do?" October was even more embarrassed, even more then last night when she had wet the bed for the first time since she could remember.

"Yes I do. There is a place at the border of Plymouth and Hellowton, just a few miles towards the very edge of it. A book hop that lets you take books for free, it's old and I don't think anyone knows about it except me. But now you do too."

"A book hop?"

"You'll see what I mean when you get there-if you go there." Sophia straightened her shirt when she let go of October and took two steps back. "Well Mrs. . . . ?"

"Blu. October Blu."

"Well Mrs. Blu, I might see you around. I have to get going, this belly isn't going to feed itself. "Then Sophia disappeared into the crowd of people passing by. A trick she must have mastered somehow, somewhere, like the Big Shop rats do when they have spent most of their time here.

Curiosity was what that girl had left in Octobers heart, like bees in the beehive, the wondrous thoughts of finding a copy of Dr. Sleep buzzed throughout her mind. One thing she noticed about the sudden meeting with the twelve year old the whole time she never smiled once. Like a straight line was drawn on above her chin when the spoke. Now she was gone, probably talking to another stranger somewhere.

October didn't want to go home, and she was done with the book section. Dr. Sleep had to be read, had to be finished. She made up her mind and was going to go searching for it. Back to the elevator she went, moving to almost a jog, making her bags and purse move back and forth.

The elevator closed her and nineteen more fellow customers inside with her. With golden luck, the security officer had pressed the floor button, just where she was heading. A full tank of gas and her list crossed off, she had finally regained the ability to smile herself.

That was the last smile October ever had.

CHAPTER 7

RAKE HAD FINALLY CLEANED out all the corrugates and replaced the water gates on the tube that was set up in field number 5. But he did notice three quarters of the way down, that there was a hairline crack in it that traveled well onto the very end.

"God damn beasts!" Rake kicked the thing. "Why? Why of all days do you have to do this to me?"

Gophers would get inside through the water gates, and cause them to break open further causing a problem further for the poor farmer. He wasn't in a great mood either, barely any sleep, hungry, and a little down in the dumps. October should have seen reason that he was only looking for her best interest, by getting rid of that darn reading. She would get some more books, but did she always have to read horror books?

He would have to order another one from Fred's Shack Goods, a market over in Hellowton that sold only handy tools and parts for farming and other machinery. Fred was an old friend of Rakes, and such a storyteller, that anyone would take time out of their busy lives to listen for a few minutes. Rake did need to get this problem fixed and replaced, but also he needed someone to vent to.

Even though he lashed out at his wife, she did still have his heart, one that he wasn't in a hurry to get back from her. He didn't want to call her, but talk to her in person, because true emotion is in the eyes. Something that he wanted to see when he apologized to her, but it was still too early for his courage.

He spit on the ground and wiped his brow with his handkerchief, before heading towards the truck.

- - - - -

Fred was sitting behind the counter with his nose buried in the Saturday paper, reading about the top ten things you need to know now. He always got a kick out of them, like how they talked to the people like they were children. Fred was far from a child by fifty years, a grandfather to seven grand babies, and a widower by almost nine years ago.

His focus was on the paper, and every now and again he would steal a glance at his employee's rear end while she worked the shelves, placing tags and making it look nice in appearance to the customers that shopped there. If he was her age, he would have had a grand time trying and eventually sleeping with her, in his opinion. He hired her on a couple of years ago as a cashier, but a girl as beautiful and fit as her, he would have thought she wouldn't have stuck around as long as she did. She had no boyfriend, and was early almost every day.

It only took a week of him training her and she was right as rain, and totally rocked the sexy country girl that wore the work apron style perfectly. It was a giant surprise when she had asked if she could have full time hours and a small raise after six months of labor. Ruth was her name, one of the daughters of Richard Figgs, and a bright young lady for only being twenty-five.

She made him feel like he was in his late twenties again, the way she talked to him and made him feel like they were buds. He knew all about her even before she had submitted her application to the store. Her mother Elizabeth had been in a tragic car accident that was caused by not paying attention to the road, all because she was too busy texting and driving. She was the reason they had passed the law in the county: to not text and drive. Some say her mother's death was a heroic blessing, to stop bad drivers around the surrounding areas and in the small towns. Fred hadn't missed a paper, and read everyone cover to cover, one that featured the accident.

Ruth was a local celebrity and so was the Figgs name. But not in that way that everyone wanted to be famous, she had lost a mother and was now half an orphan, like her three sisters were also. But she learned to keep her chin up, and somehow still be her laughing and hardworking self. Sometimes he worried about her though, but he didn't dare ask her about it, in fear of losing her as a reliable worker.

The bell above the door had rung when someone had entered his shop; it did, and almost made him jump out of chair and onto the floor. He caught himself though and folded the paper and greeted his regular customer.

"Rake ye old critten. What could I do fer you?"

"Well, I came for some tubing. Those damn animals keep using it for a house and have cracked it to trash." Said Rake. He already had his bank card out and ready for the swiping.

"What size would yer like? Don' be asking me for the larger tubes, because I'm all sold out and wouldn't' be getting any in for a few days or so."

"Those would be the ones unfortunately." Rake gave an exhausting exhale and replaced his card back into his wallet. "Well I guess I'm going to be calling it a day then, that's all I had been planning for today. Sucks when you only have a handful of fields to manage, and all it took was a crack to send me back home."

"Why wouldn't' you be wanting to head off to yer home?" Fred raised an eyebrow with sincere concern.

Before Rake could answer, he had called for his female helper. "Ruth my girl, could you watch this counter while I speak to Mr. Blu out back? I'm in dire need of a cigarette."

"Yes sir." Ruth had set her tag gun down on the shelf, to mark her territory so she wouldn't forget where she had left off. "You know that's going to kill you boss."

"You shush yer mouth this instant Missy. A lot of things can kill you in this world, and I'm already at the end of my rope." Said Fred. He had opened the counter top so Rake could pass on through the other side. "I'm just going to have chit and I'll be back. Can you handle it?"

"Oh I don't know boss. I might need you in like a few minutes because of all the customers." Teased the twenty-five year old. "Hello Mr. Blu, see you in a few minutes."

"That's my girl; give a cry if you do need my help." Fred opened the back door to the shop and closed the door behind them.

Outside there were only five steps that were right outside the door and nothing but pure cement. It looked like a basketball court, made only for some hardcore players. It wasn't a parking lot where he and Ruth would park their cars, but a flat stone garden that shined radiant gray colors. Right across from the back of the store was the Hellowton High School that was filled with teens that were on their lunch break. They were far enough that they could hear only mild laughter and quiet conversations.

Fred lit himself a cig and took two long drags from the white stick. He didn't take his eyes off of Rake when he did. All Rake did was sit on the steps with his head down, waiting for the store owner to do his talking.

"Something is bothering you Rake me boy. Yer've shopped at my store long enough, that I can read the signs. Everything okay at home?"

The old man was good. Rake guessed it was just the wisdom in him, brought on with aging and long hours of helping people with merchandise. "Yeah . . . and the Mrs. had a little spat last night. Over something stupid, but it was me who had been asking for it."

"Why would you be saying such a thing?" Fred almost chocked on the smoke that he so loved. "There is a reason for everything, ye know? Whatever you must have done might have done some good, and sometimes arguing is the best way to fix a problem."

"Well it wasn't really an argument that started it all." Rake had told Fred the story about how he had October, and how he had destroyed what he thought was the cause of her episode. "Now I'm here trying to buy some farming parts, that you don't have, and I really don't feel like going home."

"That there is a tale me boy. Sounds to me that you did the right thing-could have handled it a tad better, but I think it will blow over." The old man took another hard drag that finished off the cigarette, but before Rake knew it, he had already lit another one. "Why don't you go home and fuck your wife son. That there make-up sex does wonders, it does."

"That is another problem; I haven't had any sex for quite a few years now. It seems that she doesn't have any interest in it at all. I get shut down when I try, and she never had to try in her life."

"That's no good, sex isn't all of a relationship but it sure does put some spice in it for ye. If my wife were still alive, you bet yer ass I would be spanking her ass." Fred was pointing with his cigarette with one eye closed, showing that he wasn't lying or assuming. This made Rake laugh. For a man that had a more than a few nails in his coffin, he sure was witty and funny. "Do you still love her?"

There was a long pause. "I don't know anymore. We live two separate lives it seems. I leave before the sun, and go home after the moon is already in the sky. In the winter, she just talks about all the books she's read and the ones she *wants* to read. Occasionally she'll watch some television, but it's only that one Wizard of Oz movie that is recorded on the receiver."

"Receiver?"

"It's a device that can record shows, so you can watch them later. But that's beside the point. I think I have just fallen out of love with her."

That comment came to Fred like a needle in the eye, he knew people had problems and dealt with them in different ways. But never had he heard someone say something like that. Perhaps he was old fashion and even though he felt like leaving his wife at times, he always stuck around because he grew a heart and found that he was still madly in love. Rake on the other hand, told the truth and looked like he was going to exercise his right to a divorce.

"Well Rake, I think it might be time to change the subject." Fred had a keen eye for reading people's true feelings and desires. He had nothing else to do but run an old shop and stare at his employee's ass now and again. So a change of talkative scenery was in order. "Have you talked to Richard lately? I haven't seen him for a long while now, it be about a few season give or take. Word is Ruth in there hasn't barley seen her dud and has been raising her sisters like she was the new mother."

Richard was Rake's best friend since high school, but ever since his wife's death. The man became a workaholic and a borderline alcoholic, and had cut ties with everyone it seemed, even his own family.

"I've heard that too. But, sadly I haven't heard anything from him. The telephone goes both ways, and I've done my fair share of calling him. I gave up last year and haven't seen him since." Said Rake. The color seemed to be back in his cheeks.

"You know me friend that Ruth in there has had her eye on you for quite some time." Fred flicked his butt at the road and was already smoking a third. "How do I know you say? Experience of an old timer, plus look at yer, you look like a car with two legs. She's been staring out the window this whole time at you. Don't look or she'll be on me for snitching, but, I don't reckon she knows I know."

Rake's cheeks were red as blood, and could easily be seen through his beard. Ruth was such a gorgeous girl, and to even think that she was out having sex was unheard of. Still he knew she wasn't a virgin, on the account that she had almost every guy breaking their necks to look her way. The question was: how come she didn't have a boyfriend?

"You honestly think that she has the hots for a man of my age?" Asked Rake. He sounded flustered.

"I know it. I would be careful with that, falling-out-of-love talk around her. If you play your cards right and figure out this spat with October you could have her."

Sure enough out of the corner of Rake's eye he could see the blind move in the window, like a woman was peeking out at two men, engaged in storytelling. He looked at Fred and shrugged his shoulders. "Well my old timer friend, let's see about ordering me some tubes. What do you say?"

"Sounds good to me."

- - - - -

October had never really been on the outskirts of Plymouth before, so it took her about an hour to finally know where she was going. Past all the fields of corn stocks, and few pumpkin patches in there restate. She came upon a gravel road that seemed to have appeared like magic before her, and it was leading her towards a mansion.

She didn't know if it was a mansion or not, because she didn't know how many rooms made up such a house or how many floors it had either. But this house screamed big. The top of the house blocked out the sun, and she was engulfed in its shadow.

It was green with a white trim that gave it a feeling that it was loaded with cash or at least the owner was. There wasn't a cobweb or nick in the house's structure in sight. An expensive doll house that was titanic, it was a wonder how she couldn't see it from the road till she was upon it.

October parked her car in the middle of the gravel parking lot. Sitting there twiddling her thumbs of what to do now? Not even sure if this was the place the girl was talking about. October could have easily given up on the whole mission and headed towards home, but an inviting white sign was shining its message at her. It was written across the entrance for all to see, but not from where October was parked so she was having a hard time.

Damn old age, she thought. How could something simple as reading, act like a chore when you're on your way to the grave.

No choice but to get out and have a look see for herself. She did just that, and turned the car off and shut her door. Her footsteps crunched as she strode along the gravel path to the mysterious place she was informed to visit.

There was no sign of any life at all but her, this house looked like a clean corpse that gave off the impression that it was in an eternal sleep, and then passed away in death. It seemed to have an eerie music to it that October made up in her head as she went.

Right above the green door, was a camera that filmed her debut. Despite the cleanliness of the house, these recording eyes looked like they only filmed in black and white. She knew this, because the colored ones were hidden and out of sight and blended in with its surroundings.

These ones stuck out like a hitchers thumbs on the side of the road. Whoever was home, was definitely watching.

The Broken Pane

Was what read on the door, a title of a book she had never heard of. This had to be the place, it sounded like a book, and felt like a bookstore. But October couldn't shake the feeling that the owners lived just in the back of the Pane, but she was almost there, just like the ending of her book and wasn't going to leave until she had some answers.

The doorknob was a thick ball of silver and was a cold handshake. October took a breath and stepped into the Broken Pane.

CHAPTER 8

THE FIRST THING THAT October noticed was that there were more cameras. One was set up on top of an empty counter only a few feet in front of her, and more shared the same cable that traveled up the walls into all corners of the room. Also there was a maze of bookshelves that made it impossible to see where the hop ended. She felt like she was in the Beast's library from that Disney movie; a fantasy that only existed in movies was now a reality.

Apparently, the owner had an obsession far greater than her own. Even the floor she walked on was cases of bookshelves buried in the grown, which held books in their stomachs, covered by a glass that was thick enough to walk on. October was more impressed, and then she thought. There had to be at least one copy of the book she wanted, somewhere.

It was clean just like the outside, but she counted fifteen cameras to the one when she first walked in. Good intentions was what she had, but she could understand that this iceberg of a collection was worth keeping, (you wouldn't, play chess with a missing pawn). She only wanted one, but there was no one in sight that managed the place, so she was forced to search for it in this puzzle. October entered the maze.

Every book had a story that needed to be read. Feeling torn, she passed a lot of books that screamed to be read, but maybe when she was finished with her one, she would come back and give these novels a chance. A grand majority she had never heard of, and it was not like they were labeled by genre or author either, she found herself picking up every other book and seeing its contents. One title she read had no author's name and no picture cover either, only a title: *The Yellow Bike*, a curious one but so interesting. Another she had pulled off the shelf: *The Sand Bout*, written by: Unknown. This one had a brown leather cover and had a trace of classic in its name.

The reality was that she had never heard of any of these, and was desperate to find someone to point her in the right direction. Like the floor, the ceiling was also filled with literature and it overwhelmed her to the point of exhaustion. **Where to start?** She would just have to pick one up and start from there, if she wanted to even attempt to put a dent in the collection.

When October was deep in the ocean of words and artistic ability, there was a screeching sound that was coming from the walls, like she was right next door to a movie theater that had a boy riding a bike with some rusty gears, or had sports cards in his spokes. It could be that she was hearing things, but it was beginning to become more frequent and was grinding October's teeth.

The screeching sound was becoming a much louder ringing in October's ear, causing her to have second thoughts about even coming here in the first place. She pressed on, regardless of the shivers that climbed her spine, still looking for Dr. Sleep. Instead she found a door that was closed over instead of shut. Perhaps another addition to this already giant room? Maybe the information room? Or, the room to where that high pitched sound was coming from?

She poked her eyeball in the crack, and found another red eye of a camera looking back at her. No surprise there, the whole building must be filled with them, that much was obvious now and old news. This had to be another addition to the already giant library; all the books couldn't be contained in one room. What kind of collection would that be? With this in mind, October continued through the door without calling out to anyone. Whoever was watching would eventually know that she was lost and would give her some sort of help or advice.

This was the only door (besides the entrance) that didn't have any books in its belly. It opened into a long hall that was lit by candles instead of bulbs which were secured in a glass cover. Those walls also matched the Broken Pane's contents. October thought it was fair game to go inside, considering if it were shut, she would have just moved along and went on searching.

Portraits of iconic characters from the classic stories that she so consumed in her wondering mind, were along the glass cabinets, (painted with such detail) had made them look like there were alive. She could see Dorothy and Toto skipping along the yellow brick road towards the Emerald City - October swore she could have seen her skipping in real life; right before her eyes. The original book cover of the first book of Harry Potter, showing him reaching for the golden snitch was on her left. She admired him so much; it now was a tossup of Stephen King and the young wizard, of who was cuter.

The Mad Hatter was telling Alice it was his birthday at the tea party. Another showed the Two Towers standing in their glory, towering over the fellowship. It was beautiful. October spent a moment or two scanning the artwork with such excitement. She wished so much to have the ability to paint; maybe even Rake would accept that obsession over reading.

It was only a few moments that October had forgotten the piercing screech that roamed the halls. She was so entranced in the decor of the mansion, that when the owner of that God awful sound finally showed up. She was caught completely off guard.

The eyes resembled the red of the cameras that she had grown immune to, was now in fleshy sockets and was fixed on her every move. They had found their mark - confused at first - then was instantly ready to sound the alarm, the alarm that this intruder that walked on two legs needed to be removed.

October had never seen a pure blooded Doberman before. On screen they were always portrayed as the junkyard dogs, or used as weapons by gangs that lived in the darkest parts of the neighborhoods. The beast was stopped in its tracks and gave a glare of cruelty, he was all there but it was dragging something behind him. Better something was attached to him. The way he moved towards her with a snarling snout, he scooted with such ease across the glassy floor. Wheels instead of back legs it traveled towards October.

She stared back in a frozen state, there was never a time that she planned on seeing such a dog and never wanted to, but here it was. A cyborg of metal and fur, with all the things in the world it was tossed aside with the abominations and decided to live here.

With all these cameras, someone would have come to her aid. She hoped.

- - - - -

Rake had gone over and over, of what he was going to say to October on the drive home. He was going to try and rebuild the bridge that he had burned down, trying his hardest to make it right somehow.

The blue truck pulled into the driveway to find that the Honda was missing. No wife was home to give sorrow to. "Fuck!"

He forgot to shut the door and stomped his way towards the horse trailer, to see if October had done the one chore that he had always pushed her to do. Sure enough, he had come to find Bruno and Einstein tied up without food in their dishes, this time it felt like she did it on purpose for the way he had treated her.

"Damn wench. Did mamma forget to feed you again?" Rake stuck out his hand and scratched his babies behind the ear. They loved it when he did that, their whole bottom was wagging with the strength of their tail. "Well daddy is going to see if he can fix that problem."

Behind the trailer was the bag of dog munch, and he had loaded their bowls to the brim and then some. Hell, he even poured the whole thing out, making the bowls heap. They had enough water, but the food was what they wanted most.

"Daddy will undo your chains and let you run that off when you're done."

Then he planted himself at the bottom of the porch stairs, and chucked his boots behind him as he took them off. *Why can't she remember a simple task?* He wondered if they had real children, would she have treated them the same way. A question that he would never get answered for as long as he lived.

When Rake went into the house, he found that she had cleaned up the broken glass and the remains of the book he so hated. He knew she couldn't help herself with the cleaning, something he could have done while she was gone, to somehow redeem himself. If you make a mess, you should always clean it up. A life lesson his mother had taught him, but he could never put it into practice while married to her.

A nap sounded just fine. The fight was big enough, that he could take a few hours to himself and ponder the future conversation he was going to have with her. Where could she have been? She couldn't be shopping this long. He tried his best to make amends, but she was nowhere in sight, probably having the time of her life somewhere.

The bearded farmer plopped down in his recliner and clicked on the television, to find that October had left her cell phone on top of it. There went that other conversation, the simple phone call that led to make up sex. He closed his eyes and listened to the shitty commercials of advertisement, as sort of a slang music melody. It was only about twenty minutes that he had fallen asleep.

- - - - -

October had fallen over her own feet at the sight of the hound coming towards her. This could be considered running, but more like it was a mini train that came at a decent speed for its disability. She held her purse in front of her like a leather shield, and her buttocks hurt from the way she landed.

"Horac, boy! You behave yourself this instant son!" The screeching sound had stopped and so did the snarling. Like a light switch, the nightmare was over; all that remained was footsteps and minor panting from the dog now named Horac. "You know better than to be wandering in these parts of the house. Your master is going to have to give you a timeout for your disobedient act." A small whine escaped Horac; that was all.

She pulled down her purse and peeked over it, to see what had stopped the animal from mauling her. A gentleman was standing with Horac at his side; his right hand was like a strong leash that kept him from coming at her once more. He was an older white man with a curly mustache that had red strands of hair, tucked inside a white billow. The man dressed like he was taking her to a Ball of some sort, perhaps the butler of the house.

"Its okay miss, Horac will not harm you. He only wanted to give you a greeting that is all. He never comes over here, but your scent must have sparked his curiosity." There was kindness in his voice. He talked like he was her grandfather, and he was wondering if she was alright. "My name is Henry Fredrick, the keeper of the house and service to the owner. I had taken my eyes off the monitor for only a few minutes to get dinner prepared. Who are you? Might I ask?"

October had gotten to her feet, realizing that her fall wasn't as severe as she had led on in her mind. More scared then hurt. "I . . . didn't mean to trespass. I was only looking for a book-

"A book . . . you say? Tell me your name and I will help you with your request my dear. Forgive me, but, my mother always said it isn't polite to talk to people that won't give their name."

Fair enough, thought October. "October Blu, sir. Like I said, I wandered into the wrong part of your beautiful house, and was found by your . . . Horac."

Horac wagged his tail, (what was left of it) at the sound of his name. "Beautiful . . . absolutely beautiful name miss. So you're a reader?" asked Henry. A smile had stained his face.

"What?"

"A reader. Someone who reads as there joy and hobby. That is a grand quality to have, I am a fan of you miss October. The owner would love to have your company in the main room, we were just about to sit for supper, and you are more than welcome to join us. Would you?"

October's eyes were wide. "I . . . I can. I don't want to feel like I'm intruding, even though that's what it looks like."

Henry put out a hand that swatted the comment away like a fly. "Oh no problem, we insist; truly. The master would like to have a word with you. He is quite the talker; all he has is me to talk to and that last for only a short amount of time. He would be tickled. Please say you will."

The man's face was coveting the right answer that a drop of sweat had escaped the hairs on the top of his head. October didn't really have choice. It was the least she could do, to get out of such an awkward situation and he might be able to give her the location of the book she so desired. "I will."

"Yes!" Henry made fists in the air, like his favorite team had scored a touchdown. "It will be right this way reader." Before he had taken a walk with her down the candlelit hallway. Henry had removed the harness from Horac, and then carried him like a baby as they went. Horac looked like an innocent child without his wheels on, then a growling, screeching, and biting machine. That helped calm the nerves.

There was another door that was standing wide open, with the smell of taco meat mixed with a strong citrus, that must have been the fresh lime that was tenderizing the beef. Tortillas were the most dominating aroma in the kitchen, making the house feel like a restaurant out in the back roads of Mexico. Henry out shined October in cooking by the smell alone, hands down.

"Do you like Mexican food reader?" Henry had moved passed an eight burner stove and set Horac in a bed on the floor. October stayed two seconds behind the wondrous cook, as he went into the other room, where she found where all the cameras were connected to.

"I do." She couldn't help herself. October turned down one of the pan that had the meat in it, so it wouldn't char so much. Men loved their food a little burnt, calling it black flavor.

Henry put up his hand to make her wait a moment while he talked to someone in a chair that was in the middle of all the screens that documented the many different rooms. Suddenly, a hand poked out of the side of the chair and clicked a remote to the receiver. All televisions turned their stations to the live feed that they were present in. In the middle was a colored man that was graying in the hair and had many wrinkles around the eyes. His eyes were fixed on the female that waited behind him.

"A reader you say?" His voice was deep, like a king that talked to his court. "Well, have her sit by me. Bring out the nice china, and make her feel at home."

"Sir, she is standing right there, you can behave yourself and talk with her. I will not be the messenger for you, while you have a great set of pipes." Henry moved from his master and went back into the kitchen to fetch ware for the party.

"Come sit down reader. There is plenty room to sit and visit. My name is John Silence, and I adore your company." John was talking into a camera that was hidden inside a flower pot that held a rosebush. He could have easily turned his head around and told her, but he gave off the vibe that he spent most of his days; sitting in his chair. "Please don't mind the video footage; I have a deathly fear of not knowing who my attacker is, so I must have these extra pair of eyes. You'll soon forget that they are there."

October came around to the side of John's chair and sat on a small couch, with red interior and white designs. John was cute for an old man, give or take a few pounds, but she would've looked passed it if she was any other girl. "I didn't mean to wander in your gorgeous home sir. All I wanted was to find a book."

"That you did. We've been watching you since the moment you set foot in the Broken Pane. The name doesn't really have any real meaning to the bookstore, because it isn't a store at all, the complete opposite. It's a place where you can have all that you desired to read, free of charge, hence that's why it is a book hop and not a shop." John spoke to her as if he'd known her all his life, he liked that she sat and listened even though she was a complete stranger.

"I have been given a fortune that was passed down from my great grandfather's grandfather. With each generation from then to now, it has doubled and now will end with me, because I have no children. Do you have any children reader?"

"I don't have any." October admired John for giving her the spotlight. Surprisingly, he made her feel comfortable with his voice alone. She could tell he enjoyed storytelling. "My husband and I tried for a while but never could bare. It's my fault, my lady parts aren't working the way they should."

"Don't be sorry, reader. God has a path for you, like he has for all of mankind. I was blessed to have been born with a silver spoon, some kids take for granted and waste their money - not I - I used it to secure a home, and buy a home for all the books I can get my hands on."

"I had no idea there was a house this big out in Plymouth, and I've never noticed it before." October switched positions of crossed legs, to right over left.

"My dear, either something was there the whole time or it never existed in the first place. The house is a bit large, that it intimidates the surrounding area. Hen and I have boughten a lot over the years, which we need not leave the house. All the more time to read. I have just finished reading: *The Man That Could Not Die*, a tear-jerker at its finest." John leaned in his seat towards his visitor, a sign that he was excited to be talking to someone else for once. "We've read everything that has been put out in the world-

"Not everything sir." Henry had brought a platter of tacos, and placed it on the end table next to October. "My master likes to bark up a large tree and say that he has caught it. We've read a lot in our lifetime reader."

"Hen, basically we've read the stacks of the world's words and then some. It means the same thing. Knowledge is power, and that is the cold hard truth. Horac is the proof."

October was given her meal. While she took a bite, she glanced at the hound that was propped up on his stump, begging for a bite of that delicious taco. Henry could cook for her any day. "How is Horac proof?"

"Henry here is a retired surgeon. I scooped him up while he was at the end of his practice. When he wondered why my dog was walking lame, we tested his legs to see what the matter was. Cancer was attacking them with its sharp ax, making the poor pup have twigs instead of legs." John answered.

So we found a book on how to remove the legs and give him the ability to walk. We did the surgery here at my estate, Horac hadn't been happier with us. He would have wagged his tail if the cancer hadn't taken that too." John broke his taco in half and threw it to Horac. It landed a few feet from his bed; Horac put out a paw and pull it towards himself, devouring it. "The cure for cancer is out there reader. But you have to pay for a piece of paper that says you know it, even then it takes years for someone to take you seriously. Money wasted it seems."

October had herself three helpings. She would have loved to stay longer, but it was getting late, and Mr. Silence would have talked her into a coma if she didn't intervene. "I am very great full of your generosity John. But, I have come here looking for a book, and was wondering if you might have it."

"What book do you seek reader?"

"Dr. Sleep. It is quite new; it's on the bestselling list already and the chances of getting a copy in this small town is slim to none it seems. This would be the last and only place it could be."

John grew quiet, and then looked at his employee with searching eyes. "Hen? Might we have a copy of a book with that title?"

"I believe not. We haven't had a reader for quite some time; she would be the only reader in over five years."

"My God. Five years? Have you switched the tap-?

"No need to worry sir. There is a fresh disk in the recorder almost every three hours."

"Good." John exhaled with such relief, that a tear had escaped his eye. He wiped it away. "It looks to me that we do not have the title. We only read the ones that people leave here and the ones that we have found throughout our lives. Quite a few. I hate that we have disappointed you Mrs. Blu, your company has been water to the thirsty traveler."

A rock (it seemed like) had fallen in the pit of October's stomach as she finally got her answer. A low blow to the lovers of literature. She now had no choice but to wait the long months to finally know what happened at the end of the story. October said nothing for a long while.

"I guess I'm going to have to accept the fact and move on. I can reread it when it becomes available." She finally said.

"Mrs. Blu? We aren't going to let you leave here without a book in hand. You may have one book from our collection of your choice; it will be a real treat from us to you. That is the least we can do for such a beautiful reader like you. "John's eyes were filled with a shiny gem. They wanted to give her so much more.

October stood up. "I think it'll have to do for now. I'll read from your library. Thank you so much for helping me."

CHAPTER 9

THERE ARE NEVER ENOUGH hours in the day. Eight hours takes eight hours to complete, and man was never supposed to work at night. All this, Ruth Figgs knew. She had been a hardworking woman since her mother died and left her as the main woman figure of the family. Sure, her father worked just as hard as she did to keep a roof over them, but that was it.

Forty hours at the Victoria Bookworm Library - or the VBL - and he would come home, put the money on the kitchen table for bills and food. The rest was donated to the Answers Bar, located in the basement of

Big Shop. The VBL was one of few that weren't part of the huge market, but if Big Shop felt it needed a library in it, it would soon expand and accept the tiny library.

Ruth's father would be drowning in his sorrows; over their mother after work, while she played mom to her sisters. Their father hadn't quite given up on them, but it was an absent that the girls grew used to. The worry about where their daddy might be all hours of the night soon became the norm and the girls finally came to terms that he was still having a hard time. For nine years, they were almost orphans.

Elizabeth Figgs' death also was very popular, it would inspire the modern technology, they knew today. Cars now had a hidden signal built in them, which froze a cell phone during the time a driver would be in the car, giving all the attention to the road. The phone would be perfectly fine as soon as the driver stepped outside of the vehicle. The family would have received royalties for such an invention, but they just wanted to be left alone. It was three years ago when, society finally granted them the wish of peace and privacy.

Ruth always came home as soon as she clocked off from the hardware store. She couldn't stand the way Fred always undressed her with his eyes while she worked. A majority of woman loved the attention, despite the random out bursts of nagging; it was a secret search for a compliment that they have perfected through the generations. Not Ruth, she had given up on the prissy act ages ago, making her feel like she was an eighty year old woman trapped inside a young gorgeous body. She knew she was beautiful, but she had the personality to back up those looks, making her an eleven out of ten. Boys broke their neck almost, just to catch a glance.

Men were always on the mind, like the bees to the daisy in search of pollen, but it was more like a *man* to Ruth. That man's name was Rake Blu, a very attractive man considering how old he was. He made her believe that she was the dying breed of women, and she was the only one existing. She could have anyone she wanted, but she chose to stay alone . . . just in case. The old farmer always looked her straight in the eye while he talked to her. It was like he truly desired to know her, instead of wondering what to say next to get inside her pants.

She had just finished the last plate of the dinner dishes, and decided she too needed to be clean. The girls were locked up in their rooms, doing what teenage girls do while they are alone. Privacy was like gold to her, she rarely got it when her sisters were up and about, and the bathroom was the only place she could think. Only place to get away from it all.

The house was a four bedroom and two baths. Ruth was blessed to have a water closet in her bedroom. Rule of the house was, the oldest sibling got that room, if it was okay with dad. It always was too.

Down the hall leading to her bedroom, she moved gracefully. Almost skipping, trying to get there before one of her sisters had a question she didn't know the answer to. She made it, and locked the door behind her. A large mirror was actually built inside of the tub itself, allowing her to watch the bubbles run down her juicy breast. Something that she admired about herself above all, wondering why men love these things so much, they were just bags of meat if you wanted to call them that. Boobs were a problem for women in general; they had to be just the right size. Big enough to impress a male and small enough so you didn't have the back problems they came with. Ruth would be forever cursed with back problems, because she was almost an E cup size. A blessing for a male but a painful life for her to live.

She took the rubber band out of her hair, letting it drop down to her ass; there was a moment she was playing in front of the mirror, trying to see if she could cover her nipples with her long strands. Dark brown hair, a color she hated, but she couldn't see herself changing color. Her dad, (before the accident) would tell her she was full of shit because they also were brown, or hazel.

The mirror stared at Ruth as she stood atop of her dirty clothes, wondering what she was going to do next. She was desirable, somebody for the taking, only for Rake though. He was the one, the one that would make her the happiest she will ever be. The one that would steal her away from this Cinderella lifestyle.

A small window was above the toilet, looked over the fields of the corn, also the Blu house. It was still a ways away from the Figgs house, but when they turned on their lights at night, you could see the shadows that formed the foundation. Ruth had turned on the water, waiting for the bath to fill. She stood on the top of the white porcelain pot, and peered out, seeing the light on, only it usually isn't on around this time of night. Rake must be awake or planning to do something tonight. Mr. Blu was in bed early and up early to plow his fields.

Naked and all, she took a moment staring at the farm, fantasizing about Rake coming up behind her and kissing her neck. Perhaps even steal a squeeze of one of her girls. The light alone was making her wet, even before she put one foot into the warm bath. This wouldn't be the first time she played with herself, thinking about all the things she wanted to do with the old farmer. Ruth made herself orgasm twice that night.

- - - - -

Rake seemed to not want anything that was in the cupboards or the fridge. He had had his power nap of a half hour, and felt rejuvenated from the stress brought on by the events of earlier. Only to find his wife still wasn't home. She only left the house for a couple hours, usually in the morning or mid-afternoon, but still she was always home when he entered the building.

The Broken Pane

No friends or family, she did that to herself. Cleaning and reading was the lifestyle she chose, to want to live under a rock her entire life. Even when they decided to go on a vacation during the non-farming season, she always had her nose buried inside a book. Missing all the famous landmarks and beautiful sceneries, even to the point of not listening to what he had to say, which was always what he wanted her to do. He did that for her, regardless of what she had to say or do. Out of love was why he did the things he so deeply hated. Like listen to the constant nagging, of saving money and cleaning things that were already cleaned by her. Despite all that, he loved his wife and still did now. But it's a love that has long out done its welcome.

Rake slammed the refrigerator door. There was no cold beer in there, another pet peeve. It wasn't hard to put the whole damn case in the fridge, instead of two a day for when he had gotten home. There was only one other explanation of where she might have gone off to. She must be seeing someone on the side while he was gone all hours of the day.

"Fuck!" He screamed, because he could. He couldn't stop staring at the hole in the sliding door. Now, it was covered with newspaper and duct-tape, to when they had the time to get someone out here to fix it. She had to be having an affair. Why else would she be keeping him from knocking on the magical baby door? Because she was too busy, getting her door knocked by someone else. While he sat there on his duff, driving the tractor to raise money, so they could fuck in a bed that he slept in. Werewolves do come out during the day, only they use their penis to devour its victim's private parts.

Rake Blu had talked himself into an enraged mood. A mood that made him tear down that already taped paper, down off the glass. A kick-em-while-there-down move, one that he was unable to do to his wife because of legal reasons.

For a moment he stared at what he just did, then reaching into his pocket and felt for his keys. He was going to go to Answer's Bar. Have himself a couple of real cold ones, and maybe that food his belly was after.

He did just that.

Rake made sure that he smelled good and that his clothes weren't dirty. Heading out the door, he paused in the doorway and called out Bruno and Einstein. "Place!" Within a few minutes the dogs were waiting in the horse trailer, awaiting their male master's magic chain that kept them from running in big field.

"Now boys, daddy loves you. I'll be back with a fresh bag of dog food for you tomorrow. In the mean time, hold down the fort while I'm gone." Rake pat his dogs with deep loving strokes over their coats. Pulling away in his truck, he gave a last glance to them.

- - - - -

The Answer's Bar was known to the locals as Swer's bar, on the account that the neon sign's A and N didn't light up anymore, it hung on the door for all to see. Nobody cared to fix it, and the name just stuck and lived through times.

It was also popular to those who came regularly, for its encouraging words of wisdom it gave, in a text located at the bottom of the glass. Ones like, "You Can Do It" or "Turn That Frown Upside Down", that made the experience of drinking all the better. It went well with their signature platter of hand tossed breaded chicken strips, a side of coleslaw, and a bag off roasted honey peanuts. It was called The Original, a name that the owner was proud to have come up with himself, enough to hang a portrait of him and the food out in front of him, above the bar.

Rake skimmed the tables and the stools, to see if it was a busy night. Steady was the word he would have used, the bartender with her gorgeous blue eyes and long yellow hair, wasn't having a hard time keeping up. A young fellow with the ponytail was using his magic to woo the sweet woman behind the counter. She thought he was cute, but she was way too old for him and out of his league. Three gents and a lady were hovered around the jukebox that was playing some strong country, a taste that Rake liked to hear from time to time. A mother, towards the back, was having a conversation with her now twenty-one year old daughter.

It seemed like it was going to be a decent night. He could have a bite to eat, a glass of brew, and even see if he can give the bartender a break from the boy, give her a man to talk to.

"Hey honey, you get a man a dark draft please?" He hoped she knew what that meant. It was his way of saying he didn't give a damn, as long as it had alcohol in it. "I'll want to open a tab under the name Rake."

"You got it sir, I'll surprise you." She poked a few buttons on her computer, and reached for the glass underneath her. "Will there be anything else, babe?"

"Better get me an Original along with that."

"Dwayne! We need an Original out her!" She banged against the wall behind her.

"Better make that two. Seeing this guy made me really thirsty, I haven't seen this guy in a coon's age." A man's voice had come up behind Rake, patting his shoulder with a firm hand. When Rake looked to see who the hand belonged to, it was his old friend Richard Figgs, Ruth's father. "I was in the restroom, and then when I come out,

I get a blast from the past. What have you been up to?"

Rake agreed with what his old friend had said. A blast from the past indeed, it was only a few hours ago, that him and Fred were just talking about him. Richard was the last person he would see, especially after he had learned his oldest daughter had her eyes on him. He took the stool next to him, a good idea; otherwise he might have fallen down. "It is so great to see you Rich. I've been great, still farming and living near your house. You look like shit."

"Dwayne! We need another Original out here!" The bartender brought Rake his drink, then left her post and went through the double doors to the kitchen to see if the cook had heard her.

"There is that sarcastic personality that I miss. It's been awhile since I talked to an asshole as funny as you." Said Richard, leaning against his fist with his elbow on the counter. "You still married?"

Damn you Richard, thought Rake. He somehow knew he was going to bring up being married; it then would lead into the topic of his dead wife Elizabeth. "Still am, my friend."

"Then why are you here of all places?"

"I don't know where October is to be honest with you. She must be doing stuff with friends I guess."

"Must be nice." Richard said, his tone changed from a chipper chap, to a man with a lot of demons on his mind. "Worrying about where your wife is that is beautiful. I guess that's what you get when you become a widower, calms the nerves."

"Oh Richard, you didn't have to go there." Rake put an arm around his friend. "I don't know what to say in situations like this, please let's just talk about other things. How are the girls?"

"If I don't talk about it, then how am I supposed to move on? The girls are fine,

Ruth is watching them, she is better with them than I can now."

"You've given up?"

"No I haven't Rake, I still bring in the booty that puts food on the table and a roof over our head. Plus I'm there at night and on my days off. They're girls that need direction from a woman. They haven't had any since the accident, and they are too far grown to get the proper guidance now."

The bartender brought them their baskets of food, along with their drafts. The drinks were poured last to keep the freshness. The men quieted down while she made sure they had everything they needed, and then went to go collect empty glasses from the tables.

Richard took a long pull of his beer, while Rake sipped a bit and dove into the chicken strips that smelled of garlic and lemon pepper. He hoped that the food and drink would distract him from the topic he didn't want to hear. His friend was in so much pain, that it was hurting his heart to hear the words utter from his lips. But still Richard went on with his agony.

"I can't really move on anyways, because everywhere I go, there is always someone that is glued to their phone. Friends are being made over the internet, but they never see each other. People are talking shit right now, but we can't hear it. They're in here now, texting somebody about who they see in here tonight, that guy with the dead wife." Richard finished off his glass, the message at the bottom made him laugh. "Look Rake, it says BE HAPPY. What a fucking joke."

"Elizabeth's death could have happened to anyone. It's just a tragedy that it had to happen to you. Not to be an asshole, but she shouldn't have been texting anyways, she knew that she was at risk the moment she took her eyes off the road." Rake paused for a moment to take another bite. His stomach was being selfish, it didn't care that he was having a heart to heart with someone. "Who was she talking to anyways?"

"Thank you." Richard said, tapping his drink on the bar to catch the bartender's attention. "At least you're honest with me. Others would be the type to pamper an old grieving man, not you Rake, I like that you can be my friend after all these years and we haven't even talked till tonight."

"What are friends for? You still haven't answered my question. Who was Elizabeth texting the day she was in that accident?"

Richard waited for his new glass to be filled, before he told his story. It looked like he was going to need it. "Well. . . It was Ruth's birthday and all. She had bought her a cell phone, because she was old enough to be responsible we thought. Sixteen without a phone was unheard of in this area; we were staying with the times.

It was getting closer to the party, a small get together; the twins and Rachael were so very young. They were getting into everything and starving for attention, even Ruth was pitching a fit, about how Liz was too busy chasing kids around than helping out with party things. I was cleaning the bathroom, while Liz prepared the decor in the living room. Everything was fine.

Then Ruth opened up the gift with the phone in it. Everyone was happy, excited, and jealous all at the same time. Especially her siblings, they were pulling on Liz and whining, with that one cry that pushes you over the edge, the one that makes you wish you never had kids. That brought things to a head.

Liz removed herself from the party and took a breather outside. I followed her, leaving the kids with their aunts and uncles while I tried to calm my wife down. She wanted to kill the kids for real you know?" Richard almost finished his draft with one swig. It surprised Rake so, that his mouth was hanging wide open.

"She did, really?" Said Rake, his face had never shown so many wrinkles in his life. Around the ends of his mouth was the worst, because he was frowning at his friend's story.

"She did." Said Richard. "She had been suffering from post partum depression since she had Ruth. It was always me that kept her at bay, an escape through conversation and reading, which helped her a lot. Then one day she was getting these awful urges that she needed peace and quiet, the dead silence, if you will?

I tried to talk her into seeing a doctor, but she wasn't having it. She told me they were the problem, and they needed to go. So I did my best to keep the girls well behaved, that worked, but I could see the blood lust in her eyes whenever we sat at the table. It was sickening.

That was when I told her that she needs to leave if she can't think of any other way. I had to be a man, and let the woman that I love go, in order to save my daughters from whatever Liz was going to do to them. She called me an ass and said she was running to town to drop something off, and that she was welcomed in her family's life whenever she damn well pleased.

She got in the car and drove away. It had been hours before we had gotten a call, that she was dead. Flew through the window like a sack of potatoes and landed the front seat of the car she collided with. That driver died too. It was at a four-way stop on Walter Street, at the cross roads. The crash had an audience, one that didn't ask to see such a show; everyone was puzzled and wanted to know what caused such a wreck.

That was when they confirmed that the accident was caused by not paying attention to the road. That Liz was deliberately looking at her phone and texting with both thumbs. When we activated Ruth's phone, there was a text that came along with it, like it was from the grave or something." Richard had a tear that ran down his cheek that was instantly wiped the moment it was noticed.

Rake had eaten all his food in silence. The truth hurt so much, it hurts others. It was the first time his friend came clean, and that he was blaming himself for the death of his wife. There was nothing anyone could do to help fix his friend, and damn himself for thinking he could even attempt to give some advice. Rake came to Swers to help cope with a minor situation with his spouse, only to find that there are people in this world that have it worse than he did.

"Now it's hard to be a man, when you don't have woman to treat you like one. I'm just a person that misses his wife, stuck in a category that is under the name of: widower." Richard said, he didn't look at Rake for awhile.

"What did the text say Rich?" asked Rake. His friend turned his head slowly.

"It said . . . He Made Me Do It."

CHAPTER 10

JOHN SILENCE TOLD THE truth about; not noticing, that they were always being recorded. They were walking back to the Broken Pane, which took a lot of convincing by Henry, to get John out of his seat.

"It would be very rude if you didn't show the poor reader to the library. She is our guest, and we haven't forgotten how to treat them. Come on you." Henry had an arm around his master, getting ready to pull him up. "Sorry reader, his phobia has been caused by his father being shot in his sleep, by an unknown killer. Nothing was taken, and the trail goes cold after that. He is still out there somewhere. He-

"I can talk for myself Hen, I am not a babe." John had stood by himself and walked over to the hall, where October and Henry had to catch up. "If this killer were to ever come into this house again, I would have his face on my screen the moment he opened a window. He would be old like me nowadays, so I don't see him coming through one."

"That is a terrible story sir." October said. "I am so sorry for your loss, and I hope that criminal gets what he deserves."

"You're very kind reader." John said. He too, like October, paused in front of the portraits and admired them. "Did you see these when you came in?"

October nodded her head.

"They were hand painted, to represent my favorite books. The popular ones of course, they just make for great decoration. Don't you think Hen?"

"Yes I do Mr. Silence." Henry answered. "They put a grand smile on the house."

"Well, shall we proceed?" John offered. "It would be easier to search in the hop, then in the hall. The floor is six shelves deep; it would take a month to go through one shelf." John held the door for them, a task that was only for Henry, but they had *guests*.

The room seemed a lot smaller knowing that the two masterminds behind the operation was there to help, but was shot down. "The books are in no real order; you just have to look - read, if you will. I assure you, anything you read here will make you run back for more. I've read everything that you see here, honestly." John said, he was very proud to be the man that he was today.

October looked at Henry to confirm the tall tale. He nodded, and gave her those eyes that John spoke the truth.

"That's impressive." October said. "I've read a ton of books, but nothing quite like this. I just can't wrap my mind around it."

"You can read a ton more." John said, he made a wave of his hand to all the shelves. "We'll wait right here, take whatever you want. But only one, too many at once would make a reader like yourself go crazy."

She thought the two men were crazy - the good kind - that it was inspiring to want to read so much. She left them to bicker, while she once again went through the maze of books. Where would she start? What would she read? She had to choose soon, because it was now night, October was sure of it.

The room was well lit, but seemed to get darker while she went deeper in. Some titles caught her eye, even picked a few up, until she saw another one and placed the original one back. It was overwhelming, a buffet of food that can only be held on one plate.

Twenty minutes have passed, and the desire to read began to feel like a chore. That's when she saw something out of the ordinary. The shelves ended and a roll-up desk sat kitty-corner, between them.

What was this? Like a dandy-lion in a grassy field, it poked out noticeably. The stain on the wood was fading, and a few chips were missing from the legs, like it had termites at one point. Despite the imperfections, it looked inviting with its cover down. What surprises slumbered underneath the hood? Perhaps it was out of camera view; and John overlooked it. If he were to find out that he hadn't any eyes in this area, he would scold Henry for not doing his job.

It was rough under October's finger tips as she searched for the latch that held it shut. These old things usually required a key. She felt and looked and saw that there was no lock, but a brass button that held it all together. A firm push and the desk whipped up, making a loud squeak and a slam.

October jumped back, it took her by surprise. It could be heard throughout the building, causing the two gentlemen to stop their bickering.

"Everything alright reader?" Henry called out with his hand cupped around his mouth.

She wasn't sure. The fight this morning, the constant negative symbols on the pregnancy tests, and the let down of the book she wanted. "I'm fine, I just moved something. Sorry!" She had no idea she was so far away from the two. October looked inside.

It released an old wood polish smell, one that was mixed with a thick dust. Old newspaper was falling out, it was crammed full. It was like unwrapping a present. There was something underneath it all, October could see it. It excited her, almost made her drool. It was in the very back, easy to see with all the papers out of the way. Light shone on a single word: THE. It was a book alright, one that was away from its brothers and sisters. This was the one. A book with a mystery. ***Why was it hidden in this desk?*** October wondered.

She pulled the pearl from the clam's mouth, and admired its cover and spine. It was brand new. Bound in white leather, smooth to the touch, and with razor sharp edges. If it had been read at all, there was no sign of it.

There was no author's name or description in the back. It just had the title: THE BOSS. It was in cursive and took up the whole cover. The title was written with a darker shade of white, and a hint of red, mixed in with the cream color pages. It was cold in her hands. October felt if she opened it, the goal of leaving tonight, would never happen.

October turned to head back to where the gents were standing. Instead, she turned into John, almost kissing him. It startled her, throwing her equilibrium off. Henry was behind John, waiting for his master's next demands.

"Did you select a title, reader?" John said. His eyebrow was raised. The papers on the floor was scattered mess, it bothered the poor man. Henry was quick to sense John's intentions, and went to picking up the paper pile.

"You scared me." October had her hand on her heart. "I did . . . I found one. Sorry if it took me so long, but you have a large collection, and all."

"You're always sorry reader. It's quite funny and strange to me, is you sorry for even getting up today?" John said. There was minor humor in his voice, and smile that seemed to faked. Probably, from being out of his comfort, more than he thought he'd be. "I'm kidding. I am curious to see what you have found; maybe I can tell you if it will make you cry, happy, or scared. They are like old friends, that I haven't visited in awhile."

October didn't realize that she was concealing the book behind her back. Henry had finished cleaning, and had shut the desk. "Sir, I don't recall that I've seen this desk before. It looks ancient and smells so god awful." Henry had wagged his nose, and few red hairs had escaped his mustache.

"This house is old." John said. He didn't take his eyes off October. "Nothing had been thrown away, and it has been years since we had a spring cleaning. That thing could have been here since my great grandfather Jasper was alive, and he could have used it to hold the ground down. Who knows?"

"Yes sir, I was only making a detailed observation. Have you asked the reader if she has found the book she wanted?"

"I have asked her. She was going to tell me until you started blabbing to me about ancient history." John's eyes were sparkling with the desire to know. How badly he wanted to know, so he could go back to his chair, and sit in fear till he expired. "Shall we see?"

October handed the book over to John Silence, tucked a hair behind her ear, and waited. She didn't realize that she was clenching her fists so tight, that she was losing some feeling in them. She wanted it back, the moment it left her grasp.

"I didn't know if the desk was off limits." October said, her voice was fast pace. She didn't know why.

John didn't seem to notice at all. His eyes were like golf balls, they scanned the book, like a fine comb. "You found this in there?"

October only nodded.

"Henry, have I read this book before?" John's voice was choppy. "I can't recall. I've read everything here. How could I have missed? Tell me it isn't true."

Henry took the book from his master and examined it. Feeling it, seeing it, knowing it. Was this one that he or his master has enjoyed over the many years? Henry would know, he always knew.

That's why he was the caretaker to the large house, under the law of Mr. Silence. "You haven't sir." Then handed the book back.

The color in John's face was that of white rice and surprise. He couldn't believe that he had been lying to himself and his guest. An embarrassing turn of events. The tears were trying to break free, but he wouldn't let them. Not in front of the reader.

"She will read it fast, sir." Henry said. "Then when she is done, she will bring it back here in no time. Isn't that right Mrs. Blu?"

October was fiddling with her thumbs. She was confused. The power to pick a book that she desired was soon ripped from her the moment she picked it up. But she nodded once again. That was the one; it would be the heir to her obsession.

"I think that I will have you make another selection, reader." John held the book out in front of him, and gave a huge smile. It almost split the whole head in half.

"She will not sir. You of all people know of our policy, and that we strongly enforce it." Henry was pointing a finger at his master. "You can't go back on your word, I won't let you. So many have come and gone from here with their selection, she will not be the first to receive such treatment from the Broken Pane."

Henry spoke the truth. His outburst had brought John out of his blood lust to read, reminding him about the law which he set in motion. He didn't like it, but he knew his employee was right. John made a mental note, that he would make sure he read everything, before he made such an accusation. So he didn't miss a single one.

"I'll make you a deal reader." John handed the book back to October. "If you are as fast as Hen says you are. I will have you bring it back no longer than three days. In that time, I will do my hardest to get the original book that you were so looking for. To somehow light a fire under you."

October made sure that she had the book in her purse after that, so no more grabbing hands could get it. "I will do my hardest to sir."

"I shall live forever if I don't read that book. I don't think it's possible that I can rest in peace, knowing that there is a story, I haven't read yet."

Henry placed a hand on the back of John's neck, and then held his arm firmly. He knew that the deal was sealed, and he wanted John back in his chair before he changed his mind. "We will see you in a handful of days, we hope. With that, you should take your leave."

October followed the two men towards the entrance. John tried his best to keep his cool, he did, but his mind was pondering the thought of three days. Three days that felt like an eternity.

"One more thing reader." John finally gave into Henry handling him. "When you read that, make sure you write your name in it. A name so I can keep record of all the readers, and know that I'm not alone in this world." He smiled, and then locked the door behind her.

- - - - -

The bar's atmosphere changed. The night was indeed young, but it soon grew old, with Richards sad stories. Rake just wanted to get away, eat good food, and drink good brew. Now he felt like he was babysitting his friend, being the listening ear, and making sure that the poor man didn't hurt himself further.

"It's getting late." Richard said. "I think I've been here too long. I need to get going, it was grand to see you Rake."

"You're not driving are you?" Rake stuck a hand out to stop his friend from leaving.

"How else am I supposed to get home?"

"Maybe a cab? Your daughter?"

"I don't trust cab drivers, and Ruth is the only one that knows how to drive. She'll have to bring the lot, and it is way too late for the whole family to be up. Plus, I don't want them to see me like this."

Rake was shocked. Richard was a mess over the death of his wife, and here he is putting his life in jeopardy. On *purpose* too. It made sense now; he wanted to be with Elizabeth. But was too scared to do it with a sober mind. "I won't let you Rich, I'm taking you home and that is that."

Richard placed a hand on the shoulder of his tree-like friend. "That is why your one of the best of friends I have. Thank you." He even moved in with a warm embrace. Rake let him, he knew that Richard fought his demons every single second. "You know, you're saving me from the wheel-barrow man tonight."

"The who?" Rake raised an eyebrow.

"The wheel-barrow man. The man that waits for drunks like me, in the shadows, prowling to take up our passed out bodies. He thinks we're dead, so he has his way with us, then takes us for a ride in his wheel-barrow. To bury us with the rest of the not so lucky ones. I think he's the grim reapers cousin. Death needs to take a holiday too."

Rake didn't know what to make of Richard. Only that he had far too much to drink. Ten to his one, it was amazing that he wasn't slurring his words. "Let's get you home Rich."

- - - - -

The big soccer ball in the dark sky was brighter than ever. It lit up the Blu's farm, like a giant street lamp. But Bruno and Einstein didn't need any light, to see in the dark. They have just finished their food, and licked their chops; the master's food was delicious. That female master never fed them, like the male one did. Very annoying and uncomfortable at times, but, the male master always made sure they didn't go starving or thirstily. Praise and hail the almighty God dog, which lived in the heavens where they were destined to go.

They would've had rest, if it wasn't for them catching the scent of the female master, approaching in that large moving thing, with the eyes that shined like the soccer ball in the sky. But, she also carried a nasty smell. It put their hair on edge, suffocating them in the process. They barfed out their dinner, out onto the gravel driveway.

Never have they smelled something so foul, so harsh, and so unwelcomed. Like ants retreating back into their hill, it invaded their snouts, and moved around and around. It seemed also, that it had a physical gas, mixed with dirt and sugar, and that It filled the gaps between their teeth. Their jaws made a crunching sound, when they bit down, to somehow help it from getting too overwhelming.

She would forget about them, like she always did. Forget and just go in the house. Please, oh please, just forget this one time and go in the house. The male master already fed them the whole bag; they don't won't that aura of evil near them. It was certain that the female master was oblivious to what she brought home.

The engine was killed and the door opened. Then a foot stepped out, then the other, causing a billow of dust to form around her ankle. A sound that sounded like plastic bags, and then she grabbed *that thing* by the hand. Before she closed the door, another pair of footsteps made the same billows on the ground. Steps like the horses made - oh yes, they knew the difference.

Of course she didn't know what she was about to hoard in her house. Humans always brought stuff home, without *seeing*, the true nature of things. Like disease, food poison, or ghosts. Animal's instincts are never wrong. Neither is a child's need, to have their parents check under their bed, to see if the monster had gone. The child knows his parents can't see, only he can.

Time was different for dogs. What was a few seconds to the humans; was six minutes in dog years. Still the unnatural behavior continued, while the animals kept themselves quiet.

Rot, mixed with water and urine, walked on two legs, into the house, with their female master.

The panting slowed a bit, knowing that they weren't in the house with *it*. If it weren't for this blasted chain, both would be far away, running to find help, if it would come. Fuck the male master; he had bigger problems to handle . . . now.

- - - - -

October felt empty and exhausted when she came home. There was a small draft form outside that grabbed her, and made her shiver. That darn quick fix she did on the door, was failing at its job. It made the plastic bags ripple on the table, when the outside breeze hit the table. The book was placed on the counter by the sink.

She found herself bobbing in and out of consciousness, while she attempted to take the contents out of the shopping bags from Big Shop. Milk that was supposed to expire at the end of September, was now expired way beyond recognition. If she opened it, the smell would be the death of her. The ribs that would have been dinner were reduced to sticks, with a black powder that swam around in the package. There was nothing left of the oil, just the empty container remained.

As if she was shopping blind, or she was shopping in a cemetery. It made October gag. She quickly gathered up the items and trashed them in the waste basket beneath the sink. What on God's earth was going on? It was all fresh; the milk maybe could've gone bad, while she was spending all that time with John and Henry. But the rest, no way. No way could this have happened without even a sign. The car would have been a gas chamber.

Too tired to find out why. Rest was what she was really hungry for, the day had taken its toll on her. She would find out tomorrow. But the book, Rake couldn't find it, because he would tear it, like he did the other one. The minor strength she had left should be put to good use, by hiding the book in a place that her husband wouldn't look to.

Up above the cupboards, in the far back is a place he wouldn't look. For as tall as he was, it still would be hard to notice the spine of a white book. She needed a chair to reach up there, and to stand on the counter, so it was in the very back. Thank god for deep cupboard space. Her head felt like it was filled with water, when she came down. It made it hard to see straight, even left the chair propped up against the fridge.

Then a long walk to her bedroom, where she found the covers over a body, snoozing away. Rake was home. How come she didn't see his truck? Must be more of that blindness from earlier. It would be a fight if she woke him up, something she didn't need now; especially right now. Leaving her clothes on, she flopped onto her side of the bed, face down. Sleep had hit her, right before impact.

- - - - -

The horse trailer smelled of fresh urine and shit. Bruno and Einstein both had let it go, when they discovered that the evil had made itself at home, by climbing in bed with their female master. Their hearts were going to pound their way out of their chests. Their tongues hung out their mouth, like a tie around a shirt, dry and dead weight. Couldn't even retract it back in.

A voice, that only dogs could understand, entered their minds. Causing them to throw themselves against the walls, making the metal groan with each impact. Like the voice had attached puppet strings to them, ordering them to hurt. Hurt each other and themselves. The bond that was so untouchable, between brothers; was now cut like butter. They attacked each other, with their claws and teeth.

Bruno broke his back, when he slammed into the side of the trailer for the third time, then was met with a bite to his eyes from Einstein. Blinding him, making him cry off into the night. Dogs screamed like humans when they were being murdered. Einstein's jaw was broken and disfigured, from trying to bury it into the metal floor below.

Now the horse trailer smelled of blood and hair, a massacre box owned by the puppet master. They lay dead near each other. At least they had each other. The voice was too much, as it was burning their brain with the words it spoke. It was a song, one that a bully would sing when it stole something from a small kid. Raising it in the air as the victim jumped for it, unable to reach it. "She's mine, she's mine. I'll have her all the time. I'm here, I'm here. I'll pump her in her rear."

It was the laughing that made them hurt. Laughing about his evil plot, soon to unfold with the events that came ahead. But they will no longer be part of the future; they have become black furniture, stored in their hiding place.

CHAPTER 11

THE NEXT MORNING, THIN clouds were doing a good job of blocking the Sun. That turned the yellow beams, into the color blue. The veil wouldn't last very much longer though. Ruth usually woke up right before it went back to its original color.

Lately she had been waking up before eight forty-five. Only because all three siblings were early risers, - God knows why - and were fighting over the bathroom. They were verbally assaulting each other with words like "slut" and "whore", when they could have just used the large mirror in each of their rooms. The bathroom is the most private place in the whole world, and each girl was going to take advantage of that.

That was when Rachael had enough of the twins, and made her way to Ruth's room. Her bathroom was way nicer, and she could have some distance from the twins. She knocked twice, and then tried the doorknob, only to find it locked. "Ruthie, can I use your bathroom? The twins are being bitches to me."

Ruth lay there staring at the ceiling, hoping Rachael would give up and use the mirror in her own room. What was the point of having a mirror in there if you weren't going to use it? She knocked harder this time, calling Ruth's bluff. "I'm tired of being in my pajamas and I need a shower."

"Hold on!" Ruth yelled. "Why don't you just jump in the shower, while the twins put their makeup on?"

"It's because I don't want people looking at me. It's perverted."

"They're your sisters and they're girls. Why is it perverted?"

"Will you just let me in?" Rachael pressed on. "Plus, there is a hairy guy lying on the couch and I'm scared."

There was a hairy guy lying on the couch? Their dad never brought anyone home with him, friend or fuck, it was out of the ordinary. Ruth got up and unlocked her door. "Who is it?"

"How am I supposed to know?" Rachael said. She pushed past Ruth. "I got up to watch television, and saw that he had taken up the couch. I didn't see his face, but his fat red beard was poking out." She turned on the water, before her sister could kick her out.

Ruth looked at her sister with a surprised look. Rachael had taken off her bottoms and rolled her eyes. "You look like a peeper when you look at me like that. Go look for yourself, he's still asleep. I think he was drinking with dad. Now get out!"

Despite being kicked out of her own bathroom, Ruth had butterflies in her belly. They were having a fit, and making her toes tingle. The smile seemed to scar her face, with how hard her face muscles were working. She then made her way to the living room to confirm what her sister had just told her.

There was a heap of blankets, wrapped around a man's body. The covers were pulled up so close to his head, his beard pushed up into his nose. Crimson hair, like Rake's, she knew that beard anywhere. He was larger than life, that made her feel like a woman in an interesting way.

Rake was out and snoozing with steady breaths. He must have brought her dad home last night, telling from the heavy smell of alcohol coming from his room. Rake smelled like coleslaw more, then he did beer. He was a responsible drinker and a great friend to her dad.

Ruth opened the bathroom to find the twins combing their hair, and applying eyeliner. They both stared at Ruth with their identical eyes and with a weird expression. Rachael was right; their looks were a bit perverted as they looked Ruth up and down, wondering what she wanted.

"Can we help you?" They said at the same time. It sounded like one voice.

"Move over, I just want to make sure that my hair looks okay." Ruth turned on the sink, and then ran the brush through it, before applying it to her hair.

"Don't you have your own bathroom?" Barbara and Ella both said..

"I just need to use this mirror for a second." Ruth said. "You two have your own, so go use it. Why buy it in the first place?"

"You don't have to be so mean to us Ruth." Ella said, by herself this time.

"Are you going to make breakfast for us?" Barbara said, right after her sister.

"That's what I'm going to do, if you guys would stop hogging the bathroom." Ruth had gotten rid of the bed-head, and now it was up in a ponytail. "There I'm done."

Ruth made her way to the kitchen. She placed a skillet on the largest burner and turned it on. She would fry some eggs, sausage, and then some pancakes. Hangovers were a nasty mess, and she couldn't have Rake feeling like shit, especially when she had him here at her house.

Of course she would cook for everyone, she always did. She also knew that this was her chance to make an impression. It wasn't much, but men loved to eat and that was what women could do for them. That and sex. She hoped that he would just know that she wanted him, making the desire more bearable. If at all possible, could Rake leave his wife for her? It was a question she asked herself on the daily. Ruth wanted Rake all to herself.

Twenty minutes later, she had the breakfast cooked and prepared at the table. Her sisters would smell it soon, and Ruth would find them at the table already digging in. Rake had stirred, then slowly sat up and rubbed his eyes.

"Good morning. I have breakfast for you if you're interested." Ruth said. She placed the plate down on the table.

Rake turned and saw the girls all around the table. An awkward sight, but the food and the smell made him soon forget. "Is that hangover food?"

"Yes it is." Ruth said. "There is enough grease in there to sober up a whole party."

The farmer got up and gracefully sat at the table with the female family. "This looks great. But I don't have a hangover, I had only one glass. Your dad had enough for the both of us."

"Where is dad?" Rachael asked. She was eyeing Rake, wondering if it was Rake's fault, their dad had drunk so much. The twins shared the same expression as Rachael did. They didn't have anything to say, they were too embarrassed when company came over.

"He's still in bed." Ruth said. "You know that he sleeps till it's time to go to work.

"I was just wondering!" Rachael snapped. "He could've have spent the night at somebody's house. He has to take care of us you know?"

Ruth gave her sister a look, one that showed her that she was just acting like a bitch, because they had company over. "I'm sorry for my sister. Sometimes she just doesn't get it."

Rachael didn't have anything to say this time. She finished eating, then left the table and plopped herself on the couch. The television was then turned to Soap Opera.

Rake didn't seem like he was offended by this. He continued to eat, and looked at Ruth casually. He didn't want to get caught admiring the size of her breasts. "It's fine. I sometimes get the same treatment at home, even though I own the house."

"Is it your wife?" Ruth asked.

"She would be the one. We're on the rocks right now, hence the reason I'm here."

"Why are you guys on the rocks? You two must be happy if you've been together for this long."

"It doesn't work that way. I guess you have to have bad times to appreciate the good times, but lately there has been a lot more downs, then ups." Rake looked like he was talking to his food. But Ruth understood the topic of conversation wasn't what he had in mind. "I have to go get a change of clothes before I work today. She'll be there waiting for me. I'm surprised she hasn't called, my phone has been on the charger all night."

Tiny bugs infested Ruth's core. She saw a light at the end of her dark tunnel. They must have bit each other's heads off, if

Rake had to spend the night here. "You can stay here for as long as you like. I work at one, and my dad works at two. I'll have to take him to go get his car, but you can always make yourself at home."

The twins looked at each other with their mouths open. Rachael mumbled something under her breath. She had an attitude that never seemed to drop.

"That's okay." Rake said. "I'll just get my things and say as little as I can. She is very upset with me, and I don't think she wants to say much of anything anyways."

"If that's the way you feel is right?" Ruth said, and then she got up and put her plate in the sink.

"It'll be fine. I just need to work and clear my head. But I might have to fend for myself for supper. Other than that I'll live." Rake finished his food quick, and then did the same as Ruth, rinsing his plate in the sink. "With that note, I think I'll head out now. Thanks for the food, it was amazing."

Ruth's cheeks turned red. "You're welcome, anytime."

It took Rake maybe ten minutes to have his boots on and his truck out of the driveway. Ruth smacked her palm to her forehead, how could she just say 'anytime' like she did to the customers at her job?

- - - - -

October's room was a bright orange when she woke up. She felt like she had been drugged, with the room moving on her, and the light was doing work on her head as well. Maybe she was sick? Whatever the case, she didn't want to sleep anymore. Rake didn't even wake her up when he left this morning. He must still be in a fight with her.

There were drugs above the kitchen sink that would help with her head pain. Coffee was also a must, if she was going to shake the sandman free from her. When she swung her legs over the side of the bed, the rest of her was pulled down like a sack of potatoes, that she smacked her head on the carpeted surface. Bells and whistles were exploding in her head now, and she laid there for a bit to wait it out.

It took her almost twenty minutes to roll on her stomach, like a baby would do when it first learned how to. October crawled out of her room and into the hallway, picking herself up with the wall for support. The pictures of her and her husband were knocked down as she finally came to a vertical stance, and she waited a moment before trying her legs. She would pick up the mess, when the medicine and caffeine kicked in.

Like an old lady that forgot her cane, she shuffled along the wall towards the kitchen. She must really be coming down with something to feel this way. Water also sounded good, like she had forgotten the taste.

When she made it, October threw the pills in her mouth and felt them hit the back of her throat, and almost drowned herself with glasses of water. Making coffee felt like a chore, but when she finally got it in her body, she felt accomplished and patted herself on the back for it.

She sat at the kitchen table and rested from her horrible trip from room A to room B. Soon she felt the blood pumping smoothly through her veins, and the pain passing from her head and legs. Exhaling felt so good, like she had been holding her breath the moment she woke up.

Her clothes were damp from the sweat. A shower was next on the list of things to do today. The thought of burning her clothes came into her head, because they felt dirty and gross, never had she worn clothes for that long.

It was turning into a nice day. Great weather to sit out on the porch and read her new book she got. Did she really have a deadline with John Silence? She could have it done a day early if she tried. The love of reading burned high in her soul, but she also didn't want to feel rushed. She also had to read it without her husband finding out.

That was when she heard Rake's truck pull in front of the house. She had forgotten to feed the dogs again, there was no food on the table, and she hadn't talked to him since their fight. There was going to be another fight soon. October could feel it. Now pressure was on. What to say? Should she go out there and meet him before he walked in and scolded her for neglecting the dogs for the hundredth time.

It was too late. Before she could make up her mind, Rake was in the house and had his arms crossed over his button up shirt, and was leaning against the kitchen's frame.

"Did you have a nice night?" Rake asked. Fume was slowly protruding out of his ears. He tried to keep his cool for as long as he could.

"What are you talking about?" October answered his question with another question.

"You've been out all night." A dark color was around Rake's eyes. "You left your phone here, and didn't even think about checking in. I know we are in a fight, but the least you can do is check in with your husband."

"I was out late last night, but, you were already sleeping when I got home, I didn't think it would be nice to wake you up."

"I wasn't home last night, I was out with Richard. I had to take my mind off this whole situation." Rake came off the wall, and pulled up a seat next to his wife. "So I take it my hunch of you having an affair on me are true."

"You've gone mad-I haven't been seeing anybody. I slept next to you last night."

"Someone who was cheating would tell a lie that bad. I just came from the Figgs house, to grab a change of clothes and possibly talk to you. But I can see you don't care a damn for our marriage. I bet you think I'm so stupid."

"You are stupid." October showed her teeth at him. How could he think she was capable of such a thing? "I bet you drank the whole bar last night, even though we don't see eye to eye on things, I would never do such a thing."

Rake didn't say anything. He didn't know what to say, only do what his gut told him to do. And that was to end the discussion and get his things. Time would heal all wounds. He gave a soft chuckle at her, then got up and went to the bedroom.

October let him; she just sat there staring at the empty chair. Hating men and their peckers between their legs, because that's all they think with. This wasn't her husband. He was standing up for himself, something she wanted him to do for years. But now, she regretted the whole thing.

Tears were running down her cheeks, but she never sniffled. She just cried in silence.

A moment later, Rake had his arms full with his things and practically ran past her to the front door. He could have easily just went and gone, but he just had to say something. "I didn't want it to come to this. All I wanted was for you to show me a little more attention."

October now knew she was living with the dumbest asshole alive. How dare he talk to her like that? She gave him a piercing look, and flipped him the bird. "There's your attention."

Rake gave a smile, and then slammed the door. The pictures of their wedding day came down hard on the carpet. It didn't shatter the glass, instead it caused a crack to go up between October and Rake. A physical metaphor, of what their relationship had now become.

The Broken Pane

- - - - -

The pain-pill was doing its work on her head, getting a lot of the pressure off her temples and bringing her back to - at least - an eighty percent. The coffee was done. October got herself a glass from the cupboard and poured it with such tenderness. This drink would bring her back to a full one hundred, and she downed it, despite the burning form her mouth to her stomach.

She didn't feel like cleaning and she didn't feel like eating. She felt like she needed to read. Like a fatty goes to food for comfort, she had to hit the books to keep her mind off her husband.

The coffee was doing its job. It gave her enough energy to climb up on the counter again, and retrieve the book she hid from Rake. It felt so good in her hands. She just stared at the cover and the small details on the spine, trying to know the story it held without even reading it. What was it that Mr. Silence asked her to do when she read it? Something about writing her name in it? Isn't that like the worst thing you could do with a book, by writing in it? Either way, October found herself searching for a pen to do what she was told.

When she found one, she made her way to her chair out on the porch. It was part of her ritual. She could kill almost half the book today, easy. That sudden rush of excitement you get when you're nerding out on your favorite hobby filled her with pure joy. With the pen she wrote her name on the inside of the cover.

October Blu

She was going to have to get used to this 'writing in the book' trend if she was going to continue to get books from the Broken Pane. October stuck the pen behind her ear and read the title once more, before starting the novel . . .The Boss.

The Broken Pane

- - - - -

I spent a portion of my existence in the light. Oh how it was great and universal, time never ended in my home. When I opened my eyes, I saw my father and brother. When I flew for the first time, I wept at my father's feet. My brother's hand was on my back to show me that he too had wept, knowing that they lived out of love.

My father made me the most beautiful of all my brothers and sisters. He told me that Jesus needed a brother to learn to care with passion. Father created Gabriel next to teach me the same. Next was Michael, Raphael, Hana, Thrice, Hanamiah, Orr, Micah, Numbers, and more. Till we all knew what it meant to exist in harmony with one another. There were myriads and myriads of us, all hand in hand.

Father then created a soul. Which was a ball of light, pulled out of space and time, then was placed in my father's mouth. He then grabbed a handful of dust and formed a body that matched ours, but had forgotten to add wings - I knew, these ones were different. When he finished, he opened up the nostril and blew the ball into it.

"This one I will call Adam." *My father said to Jesus and I.* "He will live in a garden I have grown and we shall watch over him."

In seven days, he placed Adam in the garden and gave him specific duties. My father's gaze was nowhere else but on his newest son. He watched as the man cared and named the animals, feeding them and making a home in the garden. Adam noticed that the animals all had mates, something that made him tired and sleepy. That's when my father pulled a rib from the son, and made the female.

"I shall name her Eve. She will be the life-partner of my son Adam." *God said.* "Be fruitful and become many." *He told them.*

He gave the humans freewill, so that they could truly love my father on their own. That was the time he created 'The Tree'. The one called Tree of Knowledge of Good and Bad, the measuring stick. The one that I knew was going to make them like us, but my father wanted their love to be tested first. It was a test I couldn't bear to have them go through, without any help. Like my father, I too loved Adam and Eve.

The angels were created with the same powers as God, only there can be only one father. We were taught to use our powers when needed, but that time never came. I was the first to materialize on the Earth, taking the form of the snake. So she wouldn't be frightened to see such a creature as I was. The human pair knew the animals well. This was how I could tell her of the test that was blindly put before her and her husband.

She was startled by my voice, because there were now three voices on the earth instead of two. She patted my head, and asked me my name.

"Lucifer." I answered.

That was the first time I spoke in a different tongue, and the first time I talked to the newly created. I told her that her eyes would be opened up to God, and that she too could be like us if she ate from the tree that stood in the middle of the garden. Adam was off tending to some sheep; while Eve processed the new knowledge she was given.

Eve practically ran to the tree and sunk her teeth in the fruit, the juices spilled out on her and the garden, like sacred blood. Her eyes were indeed opened that she called over Adam and told him of the news. He too began to eat from the tree, and he noticed that he was naked and that Eve was naked.

I spoke the truth. Their eyes were indeed opened, that they went and covered themselves with leaves, and hid from the creator. I returned home, and was named the 'father of the lie,' that I had created a lie. That started the great argument among my brothers and sister and father. So great, that I was hurled down to the damn Earth that I helped create. That was when God created 'Sin and Death.'

Now I'm here. Ruling the majestic sphere made up of water and matter, filled with the children of Adam and Eve, an ongoing party that never runs out booze, and has more surprises then an episode of Maury.

I am not alone.

The Broken Pane

A third of the heavens came with me. My siblings dubbed me the 'Next God' if there ever was an end to our existence, and shared the same fate as I did. I am the Next God, God of sinful and imperfect beings punished for something the first mother committed. Did I really start all this? Couldn't my father, one that is all knowing and all powerful, stopped this all from happening? Did God make mankind, so they could fail and die in a matter of seconds? Did I really take the blame for all that could have been avoided?

He then casted me out of my home, instead of destroying me, made me leave, because a father cannot kill his son. My father is the creator of love and is love itself. All he did was put me and the rest of his children in the corner, while he thinks of a way to fix everything. While in the mist of fixing the problem, he had also created sickness, aging, comas, consequences, and rules that are impossible to follow.

The things that I had created in my new home have been named as crimes, pre-marital sex, accidents, divorce, misleading, murder, rape, murmuring, and theft. These acts would be punished at the end of it all. All them humans do is put freewill in effect, because that was the way God made them. They were made to be misleading from the beginning.

I remember the time when more of my brothers were sent to me, because they began to see the beauty of the female humans of the earth, and had relations with them. Making the Nephilims, who were my nephews and nieces? They too were casted out of heaven, which cooled down angels. God kept the angels from materializing to Earth then murdered the Earth by creating the Great Flood. All but eight were killed off.

Starting over when Noah walked the earth, instead of starting over with Adam and Eve.

Then what's this I see? Jesus, walking the Earth like a mortal man, perfect and teaching. He came to see how I have ruled, sent by father to see if I have learned my lesson.

I approach him, and three times I try to convince him to love me like he once did. That was when he called me 'Satan'. It was Jesus *that created the Devil. We are all God's children - all are all fruits grown from the same vine, but one. One rotten fruit named Lucifer.*

I now have control of the entity called 'Death'- The Reaper, the Shade. Because my father has made the Second Death, the final blow to living. I grow tired of this back-n-forth. I have learned of a way to go back home.

I must harvest the souls of the innocent kind. The quality souls are what will give me a ticket back home. Like father put Jesus on Earth to do his bidding, I too will use you to do my bidding October Blu. You will help me back into the Kingdom, that I so covet. That way I could speak with my father and quit this war.

- - - - -

October stopped reading. Not only was it because she had heard this story before, (through another perspective) but it was the fact that she had read her name in the book. Had this book, broken the fourth wall, right there in front of her?

There were more thoughts to come. Only they were interrupted by a humming sound in her head, one that was burning like a hot iron brand. The book began to grow damn hot, in her hands, that she threw it to the floor. A force, the kind you feel when you open a heavy door on a windy day, wrapped itself around the waist of October, throwing her back against the house.

The impact was hard enough and right on the button, that it split the house and the part of the gravel driveway in half. The house stayed together, but moaned as it was dealt a wound on its old forehead. Chips and pieces of pant and plaster were scattered all over the porch, and parts of the roof, rained down into the yard.

The whiplash should have knocked October unconscious, but she was still there. She did feel like a loli-pop, sitting there in disbelief. The book lay open on the porch, making it look like it was an opened window or small trap door. Yellow and red light shown through, and with it along came fire and screams. October was hoisted up into the air, against the wall of the house; the heat from the book was burning her with its hell fire.

This was Hell indeed, the fiery pit that the dragon ruled over. The one called Lucifer.

A voice, that came from none other than the author of the book. Spoke to her from the red hole in the porch. "So, you like to read now do you?"

CHAPTER 12

IT WOULD HAVE BEEN easy to have left Rachael and the twins at home, while Ruth took her dad to his car at Swers, but the sisters insisted. It would have been easy if the girls did anything but complain the whole car trip. But these were hard times, ones that were never going to get through easily while their mother was dead. Considering the experience Ruth had with all the girl's constant complaining, she learned very quickly to drown out the noise. While she drove like a robot, one of her quirks was biting her lower lip, as she listened to her father scream at Racheal.

"Will you please calm your fucking voice?" Richard threatened her with the back of his hand. But he would never deliver it.

"Good fathers are supposed to listen to their kids." Rachael screamed back. She was always the first one to express herself.

"I do! You just know how to push my buttons don't you little girl? Why can't you be quiet like your sisters?" Richard gave a quick smile to Barbara and Ella. They returned the smile and stayed quiet. They didn't say much after their mother's car accident.

"You're a dead beat, *Richard*. If that is your real name." Rachael laughed aloud at her joke.

"You little bitch!"

"It takes one to know one. Ha!"

Richard shook his head. Knowing he had lost the word match. He was the kid now and his daughter was the adult.

"We're here." Ruth said. She missed her dad, but couldn't wait to get him out of her sight. "Thank god! You two fight more than birds over a worm."

"Whatever that means sis." Rachael was on a roll. If she had a remote to her voice, the MUTE button wouldn't exist.

"Thanks Ruth. I'll see you tonight."

"Yep, you always say that dad." Rachael said. She never knew how to keep her mouth shut when it was needed. "I bet you're going to the bar again. We haven't seen you in fucking month, unless you get bored."

"Will you shut your fucking mouth?"

"Yep, okay Richard."

"That is enough!" Ruth had given her sister a look that would have sliced the neck of the obnoxious teen. That was the final straw, and the needle and thread that sewed the mouth of Rachael.

Ruth definitely had the death stare down, even gave it to her dad at times, and it worked all the same. Women had that power over men. Maybe it was because women had the vagina that men always wanted to get into, or probably because women suffered for almost two years when they get pregnant, from the physical pain and mental stress, that formed a woman into motherhood. Richard would never think dire of his oldest daughter, but those ghost stories always stuck around in the minds of a smart man.

Richard, however felt sorry for Ruth, only because he knew in his heart of hearts that he was a piece of shit, and he threw the load of parenting on her like it was never his job in the first place.

"Just go dad. The sooner you get to work, the sooner she can shut up." Ruth said. She reached over and gave him a soft shove. Richard got out and told everyone that he loved them-even the little brat in the back seat. No one would believe it, but he loved her the most out all his daughters.

Ruth was his brains and the twins he loved but he never spoke to them and made *that bond*, the bond that caused a father to make sure perverted boys stayed far away. Racheal though, they fought all the time, but at least they were exchanging words. Ruth reversed and made her way out of the parking lot.

"Can we go in Big Shop?" Rachael asked.

"I have to go to work, you know this." Ruth couldn't believe her sister would ask, she knew she had to be at Fred's in a few short hours, but she asked anyways just to annoy her. "I'm going to go home and get ready. You guys will survive without me like you always have when I work."

The twins gave each other a look, one that they only understood, that being alone with Rachael was hell. Rachael would indeed keep them busy with her chatterbox for a mouth. Surprisingly, the drive home was quiet. That was a nice.

The Broken Pane

- - - - -

Rake found Fred outside in the back smoking his third cigarette. A fourth one was behind his ear that would quickly be reduced to a butt once he got to talking.

"He' there chap. It's only the next day, them tubes are not in. Tomorrow, only if the tube store had nothing better to do. Spit on it."

"I know." Rake said. He took a seat on the last step of the stairs. "There is nothing in Plymouth, but the tumble weeds and the need to throw up, from all the work there is to do."

"Amen, friend." Fred pulled the cigarette from behind his ear, but this time he held it out to Rake. The old codger knew his buddy was still stressing about October. "Here, this will take the edge off. I know you don' smoke, but one isn't going to make you drop dead."

"You're right, I guess it doesn't matter now." Rake took the cancer-stick from

Fred's skinny claw. Fred also had to provide him with a light, non-smokers didn't have things like that lying in their pocket. "I went to go have a simple conversation with October, but we ended up fighting again. The good thing is, I actually had time to visit with Richard last night."

"Oh? Did this meeting consist of you two throwing back some barley-pop?" Fred chuckled at himself. He knew that this was an old saying, and it would fly right over Rake's head.

"I only had one. Richard would have drank the whole place if I didn't tell him otherwise. I even spent the night with him."

"You don' say?" Fred's eyes were wide and the cigarette butt was hanging out of his lips like a kick stand.

Rake was starting to get light headed from smoking the 99, but he muscled through it. "I do say. Your worker Ruth even made me breakfast, it was quite a surprise to me. It was great."

"I'd expect her to do something like that, considering what I told you yesterday."

"Wow! I didn't even remember that." Rake looked at the ground in disbelief. "Now that you mentioned it, she was putting off a vibe of acceptance. Like she was sitting across from me, and she didn't have to cook me anything. Her sister was damn vocal about her dad and me, which Ruth was defensive about. The whole encounter felt like a date in a way, and I was meeting her family for the first time."

"I spoke the truth then. That girl is wanting to give you; or *show* you something your wife probably hasn't done in a while. She should be here any moment." Fred reached into his pocket and pulled out a gold pocket-watch. "In a few seconds the bell will ring."

Rake finished his smoke and flicked the butt towards the street. "I guess I'll get to work then. I'm not used to irragating this late in the day, plus if she does like me like that, I don't want to distract her from her work."

"Do you fancy her?"

"I'm not sure, but the way things are turning out. I become more and more attracted to her the more I see here."

Then the bell rang.

- - - - -

Ruth saw her boss and Rake come from behind the counter, but they didn't see her, she had hurried to the break-room before she was spotted. She wanted to see him again, but part of her plan was not to have him see her until she got off, that way he had time to think about her-if he was thinking about her.

She wished he was.

The thought about getting off early was entertained in the back of her mind. She may be able to, even thought she was the main focus of the market, Fred had to come in and run it himself instead of slowly killing himself out back for most of the day. She hadn't missed a day of work, or asked him more than anything but what time it was. The old man had to have some sort of passion for working, how else was he going to afford his smokes? Even if he made a hefty profit from his small business, he spent it all on tobacco.

Despite not needing a lock - because there were only two people employed - she did the combination and stored her expensive pink and zebra Couch bag, along with a sack lunch. Only this time it contained two homemade chicken salad pitas, two bags of BBQ chips, and two cans of Root Beer sodas. A generous gesture, but Ruth didn't want to come off as too forward, but at least this would break the ice between them. She was a great cook, and there is always different styles to cooking. Ruth's cooking needed to be great otherwise her family would waste the food. October only needed to cook for her husband, and if felt thrown together.

Racheal took her apron from the hook, and made sure she didn't disturb her hair as she slipped it over her head. There wasn't a major dress code for work, only the casual jeans and a polo with three buttons. She neglected the buttons, and a v-shape effect caused her shirt to show a portion of her cleavage. Fred wouldn't care, as long as he could look. He was very good at making sure he didn't stare too much, he didn't want to get a sexual harassment charge on him. One she would never insist on, because a man is gonna look. A pig is going to stare.

Her hair was down and straight, instead of the normal ponytail she wore on a daily basis, men liked to see some change in women. That way it was easier to strike up conversation. There was not much she could have done with her jeans, but decided she wasn't going to wear any panties. The idea was to look sexy, but still be casual, make it look like she wasn't a slut but was blessed with great genes. Her plan was working so far, only she would have to make sure she stayed fresh till she clocked out from work.

The thought of *quitting* crept into her head, if she wasn't granted the time off. She had a great work record, confidence, and smart to find another job soon. If it came to that, she would use the extra time to her advantage. Her sisters would still think she was at work, and that was a great thought because Racheal didn't want to be rushed while she was making a difference in her love life. It would be a drastic decision, but the end of a chapter meant the start of a new one.

What if she couldn't get the affection she longed for by the man she was in love with? A lot of women were in love with men that had no idea, but she was different. That put the thought of doubt to rest. Love is misunderstood; taking things slow meant controlling a fire. You're supposed to fall in love, and let the fire get out of control. His love will come, but first she needed to let him know of her intentions by show, rather than tell. A relationship based on sex, sometimes bloomed into feelings. This was her plan all along.

Racheal gave herself a quick glance in the mirror that hung on the locker door. The time clock showed that she was right on time when she punched in. But before she could go out on the floor, Fred was leaning in the doorway, and he blocked her way. It took her by surprise, because she couldn't remember ever seeing him step foot in the break-room.

"Yer don' have to work today." Fred said, his arms were crossed. There was a twinkle in his eye. "I'm giving yer the day off, and I will happily pay it."

"But why?" Ruth crossed her arms.

"There will be no explanation. But if yer want one, it's because I said so. And if you don' go today, I will fire yer. Do yer understand?" Fred had a slight smile. A smile that was hard to see because of his wrinkles, but Ruth saw it nonetheless.

"Yes sir. . . I . . . will." Ruth also had a smile, but hers was more obvious. She went back to her locker and got her things out. There was a minor silence, but it soon subsided. Fred offered her a hug that she willingly accepted.

"I know yer a good girl, one that has wings. Yer deserve to fly Ruth. I know one day isn't much, but this here is my damn store, understand?"

Ruth gave him a kiss on the cheek. "Thank you Fred. I'll be back on Monday, bright and early."

Fred led her to the door, when she left he put the CLOSED sign up then threw the deadbolt in.

It was the least he could do for her. Fred knew she was going after Rake - it didn't take a rocket science to figure that out. The outcome of her mother's accident, it was her family that suffered the most. But Fred's family died in that accident too, but made sure his wife's name didn't make public eyes. It wasn't any of their business, they could all piss off for all he cared. But the random questions about the death of a loved one would surely make Fred slit his wrists.

Ruth never knew that his wife Monica was the other car in the wreck. That was the main reason he hired her in the first place, knowing that she needed a source of income to support her sisters. Fred hired her on the spot, no application needed. He knew that the money he earned from his shop was too much for him to spend by himself.

When he got the call that Monica was in the wreck, before he went to go make sure it was his wife that was in the car. He bought his first pack of smokes, so he could meet her in heaven ahead of schedule. He was too scared to take his own life, despite trying. There were a few times he had a barrel in his mouth, but couldn't come to pulling the trigger. He was afraid he might survive, and he would spend the remainder of his days in the hospital.

Everyone knows that hospitals are haunted.

Monica layed on the metal table - more like a cooking tray - still and quiet. She would've looked peacefully asleep, except there was a huge gash on her forehead. The hole had been stitched together, and the blood was dried into a sickly black color. Dr. Miles stated that she had fell asleep at the wheel when she ran the red light. The impact was massive and extreme. Two drivers crashing into each other, at a steady speed - not paying attention to what's in front of them- if it could have been helped or not. The steering wheel had sliced her head open, and when the air bag deployed, it pushed her face and forehead apart. It was like her head had a huge black grin.

Fred wept at her side. Despite the massacre of her features, he still thought she was the most beautiful woman he had ever met. He loved her more than he loved himself, and the thought of living in this world without her made his soul hurt. He was a strong man, but this loss made him feel like a defenseless boy. The Grim Reaper always comes on time, but why did he have to come now? Why couldn't he come for him first? Why did bad things happen to the good ones, and the bad ones live forever?

Dr. Miles waited a good hour before pushing a clipboard in Fred's face, the certificate of death, the papers that said the doctor did his job and he could go home. Well the old man signed the papers, but mentioned that he remain out of the papers, or tell whoever wants to know what happened to shove it up their ass.

Fred went out the back of his shop, and sat in his favorite spot. He had one more cancer stick, but he knew this was no bother. He would just take another from the shelf and smoke that pack too. He lit and took a hard drag. Looking up at the sky, where he knew his wife was looking down on him.

"I'm coming Monica. One way or the other."

CHAPTER 13

THE SUN WAS IN a different position. I didn't peek into Mr. Silence's window the same; it didn't brighten up the day so to speak. Even though John was staring out the window, and swallowed up by its large glow, he had turned the color blue.

"Sir? You're going to go blind if you keep staring into the light like that." Henry said. He had layed out the clothes on his master's bed, while he tried not to mother Mr. Silence. His master was bare ass naked and pouting. "I think you would commit suicide if you couldn't read another story-

"Don't baby me Hen! I'm thinking!" John didn't quite yell, but answered in a firm voice.

"It hadn't been a day sir. She will bring the book back, I know it."

"Speaking of which, did you by chance order that book off the internet?"

Henry did just what he was told, he always did. But this was one thing that he couldn't get done the way his master wanted him to. The inventory of Dr. Sleep was sold out everywhere. Even the ads for yard sale's that advertise their stuff for sale had everything but books. He wouldn't dare go to Big Shop to check. Mr. Silence was a recluse, and it was damn rare that Henry was allowed out reach of John's voice.

Everything was bought and shipped straight to the Broken Pane's front door. The coveted book would only be three days old, it would take only a blessing for it show its self in the near future. These were the days he hated his job.

"You know the answer to that. I spent hours on the internet, combing a location of where I might find one, but there is no such luck."

"Damn!" John hit the window in front of him. It made a gay noise, but it was the sound that snapped John from his dumb state. "I don't blame you Hen. I just wanted to read as much as I could before I pass. I don't have much time you know?"

"Don't talk like that master." Henry pulled John close and held him like a teen, one that just experienced his first real break up. Mr. Silence cried onto the Henry's suit and tie, making the fresh iron job, smell like sweat and salt. "You're just going to have to read a small book to pass the time. Come now, let's put on your favorite shirt. The one that has that strange passage on it, what was it?"

"A writer writes, right? Right, a writer writes." John had stopped the water works the best he could, then went over to the bed and put on that very shirt. "Thanks Hen, I do feel better when I wear this shirt. Did you make lunch?"

"Of course I did, but its a late one, so I guess you could call it linner or something like that." Henry chuckled at his joke, and even gave himself an applause. "While we eat, I can look online again for that woman's book."

"Yes we can do that, but I would like to see the footage of that night she got out."

"Who?" Henry said, his bush eyebrow had almost touched the brim of his hair.

"You know who. Not the lady from yesterday."

"Oh my! Right right right. I thought you said if she didn't turn up in a day or two she would be dead to you."

"I did say that, but I find myself missing her. I would like to see if she left any clues of where she might have gone to."

"Well let's get you down stairs, I'm tired of staring at your groin."

"Oh...right." John picked up the slacks, ones that were a tad worn. But that was the way he like them, less restrictive, comfortable, and still formal. "I know she'll bring the book back, its just me throwing a tantrum, mostly caused by an empty stomach."

- - - - -

The feeling of having the day off – unexpectantly- put a grin on Ruth's face that only a miracle would have to change it. Her father should be at work and her sisters were old enough to manage themselves for most of the day. The plan to win over Rake with the lunch that she made him, went into effect earlier than expected, but that was okay. She had the music on blast, and her hair was dancing from the wind, as it came rushing in when she rolled her window down.

She knew where to find him too. Over at field number 6, the one before the broken irrigation pipes. In her mind she was stalking him, she was more waiting for the right moment to strike, or play the cards she's been dealt. And she had a royal flush, one that could only go wrong if she allowed it. Rake was vulnerable, and she had the looks and the tits to make him change his mind.

It was at field 4 when her nervousness sank in. *What if he didn't care? What if he lectured her like she was a teenage girl? What if he felt sorry for her, and threw her a pity party?* These were good questions, but there was only one way to find out, and that was to dive in head first.

Ruth got herself together, because she saw the truck coming into view, parked in the dirt road between the corn fields. She continued to drive on by, only so she could calm herself down a bit more. It wasn't long until she turned herself around and parked right behind the old farmer's vehicle. *Could he have heard her pull up?* It didn't matter now, considering he would find out when she went into the corn to give him his surprise.

Her engine wasn't load, but she had the radio load enough to be heard if she were to stop at a red light. Which she would have turned down so not to distract the other drivers. There was not any stop lights or cars on these back roads, only the land owners and the farmers that worked them. Even they wouldn't allow these roads to be busy. The music had Ruth's ears humming when she killed it. Rake for sure had heard it.

A few moments went by, but the old farmer didn't come out of the corn to see who had pulled up. Mostly indicating that Ruth had to make the first move into making her presence known, that wasn't hard. She was an emotional wreck for a few seconds, but she put that behind her and was pushing the stocks out of her way as she ventured into towards her desire.

The sound of a spade was being driven into the mud up ahead, it was a mystery that Ruth didn't notice that her feet were wet and cold and stuck in the ground. She took off her shoes and threw them towards her vehicle. Now her feet felt like ice blocks as she walked towards the sound. Rake of course was use to it, the life of a farmer was nothing less of hard work, the severe coolness of the dirt was nothing more than lion seeds on the wind.

What would she say to break the ice? Say 'hi' was normal, when you saw them at the grocery store. Conversation came easy when she was in her comfort zone - doesn't anyone? But this was his turf, the field that he plowed was like a palace to him. Ruth looked more like a maze made of corn, haunted by the man that she so desired.

Ruth could see him now, his back was turned and he was fixing his water trenches. there was a large puddle of water that was forming, and if he didn't do anything about it. The corn would die from having too much water, while the rest died from not having enough water.

She could tap him on the shoulder, but that might startle him, it would be funny to see. Maybe he could spot her, that way he broke the ice then having her think stradegy. The back muscles showed through a light blue button up shirt. His hair was dark brown almost black, slightly muddied jeans, and rubber boots. The problem was fixed, but it would take a while before the water reached the other end, now he was just admiring his work, and making sure the dirt mounds held up.

Ruth was wasting time, she had to do something. It would look highly unusual that she was out her by luck, that she paraded in the corn for her health. But, when she got up enough courage to say anything. He turned and looked, he had surprised look on his face, but anyone would have that look if they were in his situation. Seeing the girl that supposedly liked him, wondering why she would be in a place like this; when he just left her at her workplace.

All that he could say was her name. Almost like a question, but not quite. She stood there beautiful with a brown bag, and something to say. His name was all Ruth could say too.

- - - - -

There on the porch, was the corpse of October Blue. Her body was mangled and burnt. The parts that still had blood coming out it, was her fingers. They lay on the open book, dripping like candle wax, giving the book some more character on its white surface.

They always say when you die; you either go to Heaven or Hell -and this is true- depending on who you talk to. When you're good, you meet the heavenly father that started it all, called life. Or if you're bad, you are to be burned and tortured for all eternity. October found herself in hell, only it wasn't the burning rein of fire, like in that Johnny Cash song, oh no. She was actually way deep in her right eye, wandering around in haunted black, that sprouted thin trees, and leaves that covered the ground, like broken glass.

She of course was crying, only because it seemed that the ability to calm down was completely gone from her DNA. Dead as the leaves that covered the ground. Like skeletons, the trees made queer crunching sounds by themselves. There was no wind where she was. Where was she? There was no destination in sight, no yellow projects like in her dream she had before, just a long road with no signs or light. Even though there was no light, she could see just fine. This sudden realization, made her weep even more strongly than before. That was when she heard the voice. A voice that had no mouth or owner, not yet anyway.

"Yes. You are dead. Like me, Hell comes in all different shapes and forms. One time I found this human rolled up in a tiny ball, and yet he was breathing and screaming like it was so natural for humans to do that. He's still there."

October could hear every word, clear as the light at the end of a dark tunnel, even over her the harsh sounds she was making. It was as if going horse was never going to come. She stood there in one spot just screaming at nothing, while the voice continued his rant.

"Your Hell is the loneliness. Nothing but trees wasting away like yourself, with arms stretched outward with nothing to grasp. Like that baby you've always wanted. All the eggs and all the sperm, but not one could make it through the spider-web of sin."

Truth was what shut her up. She truly wanted a baby. Everyone else was out fucking and getting pregnant - on accident too - but not one baby; not even a fucking miscarriage. The screaming had stopped, but the tears and exhaustion was still there. She stood there on the black floor, only it was starting to get light up. Black, then purple, then blue, and back to purple again. It was only a few seconds before she realized she was standing on the pupil of an eye.

The voice was coming from that eye.

"You opened the book, and now you must accept the deal."

The Broken Pane

Octobers body stiffened like a board, making her vulnerable like a voodoo doll. She was floating in the air now, all she could do was watch and listen. As the black nothingness started to take a form that she so recognized from the horror of her dreams.

Dark violet dust and Shades of red and blue were whirling around and around, when finally a head was shaped, and the neck that it sat on was visible. Arms and legs came seconds after. It was the lumberjack that chased her in her dreams, that carried her off into the blackness of space, and called her "Gir" with that haunting voice. He resembled her husband, the one that; as of late, grown to hate and easily annoyed at the idea of him. This scared her the most of all, being roughed up by the person you knew the most, and at one time loved with all her heart. It made her die inside all over again.

"I visit often the dreams of the human race, now you have come to visit me gir! I am he -or

her- *the ruler of this world, and the one that mankind calls Satan."*

There seemed to be some thunder and lightning when he said his name. Like in those old comic book movies, when the villain was giving his monologue to the superhero.

"I would tell you not to be afraid, but that would not be possible, I take the form of what you humans fear the most. A punishment by my father, one that is annoying and useful. I can get what I want from you humans, and that is why I must have you accept the deal, you have no choice but it is rude not to ask."

October passed out, it was a wonder why she hadn't already. But even with her eyes closed, the image of the lumberjack stayed like wine on white carpet.

"Don't go running away from me cutie." And like the giant floating heard from The Wizard of OZ, telling the fellowship of the ruby slippers, "bring me the broomstick of the witch of the west!" Straight to the point,

and forced to take the deal that would change everything.

"You may keep your soul . . . for now. You will do service for me that will require you to be alive. You will harvest souls for me, that I may soon have enough to buy my way back home, up in heaven. That I might be able to tell my father sorry, and that his son has missed him so.

Time is different, it has only been two days since I was hurled from the heavens, and on the fourth day is when the second death will make his way on golden wings and a dagger in hand. No man or beast will ever return from the second death.

That being said, you October will take the souls of children for me. It is not the quantity of souls, it is the quality of them. Before puberty, the child's life is fearless and untainted from the world. You make think it is I who has made the place of the living hell. But it is actually the creation and free will of man."

Like a flash of light being turned on and seeing the roaches scatter to another hiding spot. October felt a punch to her gut, then her mouth was moving and her eyes twitching left to right. The lumberjack continued his offer, only using her body to tell it this time.

"Humans are interesting creations; they can be bought so easily. Like you my dear," October's hands came to her breasts and she began to squeeze. *"You'll say 'yes' to me as long as you get what you want. I can see it all inside you head. You'll live, be young, and have the power to fulfill what is needed to get me my souls. They weren't yours to begin with anyways. Who said you can keep it?"*

As if like a picture book turning to the next page, the scenery changed to throne room. Black and yellow knick knacks scaled the surfaces of a thousand tables. In the middle of the room, sticking out like a sore thumb was a chair, and at each side was what was left of Bruno and Einstein. They were hell hounds now, but the sad thing is, they would have died anyways under the watch of the their female master. Neglect was an evil murderer.

The Broken Pane

"Here is where you will sign." The lumberjack spoke the truth. A glass table was set up in front of the throne, that twisted and weaved like the roots of a titanic tree. The dogs were so stiff, that they could have been mistaken for ornaments. Perhaps they were, only they were alive in their new life. You named it, a contract written in gold and scarlet, that only the Devil could read. October knew that it was held the information of what he was telling her.

"Yes. You are a smart creature October, one that only needs to sign and it will be all over. You will have my permission to live again as you once were, only with a mission, and one more slight change in your physical make-up."

October's hand reached inside her stomach, without putting a hole inside her flesh. There was a pop and a twinge of pain, and it was all over. *"There you go gir. You will now have the ability to get pregnant. I have given you all that you have desired; now you must give me what I desire."*

Quite literally, having a huge weight lifted from October's chest. The Devil came out and sat on in his chair and watched as the woman held her stomach, and had her mouth open like a scream; only there was nothing coming out of it.

"Sign your name, and this will all go away. If you don't. . . "

After saying this, there was a squealing sound and the thumping of footsteps. October turned in the direction of the steps, to see the new comer. It was a . . . thing . . . pushing a wheel barrel towards the chair of the bearded black phantom. Inside the barrel was the skulls of the some not so lucky people.

"These are the souls of the humans that don't be careful when the go out drinking. This is the easiest way to get me my souls. How many times have parents and friends, told the ones that find the joy of drinking, to be careful when they go out to play. Don't they know that the wheel barrel man is lurking in the shadows, waiting to take the soul from the drunk man?"

The Devil patted the monster on the shoulder, as he dropped the skulls into a pile in front of the throne. It then continued making its way to the back to where it came from, where it went into hiding to get the next load of unfortunate people.

There was no way to describe it, no time to describe it, only enough time to sign and leave. On the table, was a pen and paper. No different from the average college ruled sheet that anyone would use to write on. The thoughts that October thought was instantly answered by the one sitting on the twisted throne. Her thoughts were his. "It doesn't need to be fancy, it doesn't need to be explained, it just needs to be signed. The rest will come fast and natural. Otherwise I can call my friend back, and find another one. You wouldn't be the first to fail, and be replaced."

What choice did she have? The stories were true about Hell being a place of torture, only a million times more than that. She would become currency to him, so he could go back home. He had that right, his father was the one that made; well everything.

She picked up the pen, and hesitated for a bit. It would all be over soon he said. *"That I did, and if you don't do it right now, I will rape you till I fall tired, but Angles don't sleep, so keep that in mind."*

A fire was lit under October's ass; after this comment. Then the deal was done.

CHAPTER 14

THE TWO STOOD THERE in the corn field for a few minutes, staring at each other like they have been lost lovers. The corn field wasn't that crowded, because Rake owned the piece of land, but it seemed to need the most work. When you are managing the up keep for someone else, you seemed to do a better job and invest the most time in those assets, than you would your own.

Rake felt like the Mr. Harvey in the movie, 'The Lovely bones, with Ruth out here all alone. But it was far from that, he felt like a grandpa; wondering why his grand child had wandered so far from the farm.

"Don't you have to work today? I could have sworn I just saw you in the shop like forty-five minutes ago." Said Rake.

"You did, but Fred gave me the day off today. He said I would need it, I get paid to do what I'm told, not to have an opinion." Said Ruth. "Plus I wanted to bring you these sandwiches for lunch. I was thinking about what you said to me at the house, and thought that things didn't go well at home like they were supposed to."

"Well they didn't." Rake scoffed, looking the other way for a moment. "The fight goes on, still not sure what to do after work. But I have to resolve it somehow. Can I take those off your hands?"

Ruth was confused of what he was talking about for a second. Then found out he was talking about the food she was carrying. She had forgotten she had them, just from the mere image of him standing there in front of her. "Oh . . . sorry. Here, they are fresh, made them right before I walked out the door on my way to work."

She walked to him, watching as Rake grew as she got closer.

"Thank you. This is the nicest thing anyone has done for me." That was a lie, but it sounded right. "Food and men get along just fine."

The old farmer tore open the plastic bag, and took out the triangle shaped sandwich, tomato juice and horse radish juiced a bit out the bottom as he took a big bite. Ruth waited to see how he would react to the taste. Plus it was a reason to look into those eyes that were almost hidden with his hat and beard in the way.

"Wow. I don't know what to say. I feel bad just standing here and eating in front of you." Said Rake.

Ruth put up a hand. "Don't worry about it. I have something to tell you anyways." That same hand she put up, came to her mouth. She vomited the words out by accident. Of course she had something to say to him, but that could've come later.

"Oh yeah? Like what?" Asked Rake. He had the sandwich finished within a few bites, and was now wiping his lips with his clean hand.

Why lie when you can tell the truth. It's not that she was digging herself a hole, how could he know what she wanted to say to him? But what is considered great courage and confidence -especially for a girl- Ruth said what is exactly on her mind.

"I came to tell you that I have been crushing on you for a long time. Forgive me for being rude, but ever since you told me that you and October were having a fight. It has done nothing but bring a smile to my face and butterflies to my gut. That's why I'm here."

It took all that Ruth had to say that. It was easy to say, but she found that a tear was falling down her cheek.

Rake removed it from her face with his thumb. They were rough, but had that touch that she so longed for. "That takes a lot of guts to say, Ruth Figgs. I'm a married man, even though the marriage has been hell as of late, it wouldn't be right to have the same feelings."

It hit her like a ton of bricks. It felt like she was living her birthday all over again.

"But 'I do' have the same feelings Ruth." Said Rake suddenly. "I'm practically your fucking grandpa and best friends with your dad. I watched you grow up, that is just nuts to say out loud, let alone to you. But I feel the same way."

Ruth looked up, that was what she wanted to hear for so long. But now that it was said, she didn't know what say or do. Rake made that easy for her, because he ran his fingers through her hair, then when he came thirty percent, she soon went for seventy percent. They kissed and kissed, special was one way you could describe the moment. Both were sexually frustrated, both needed that physical attention, and both needed to just get things out in the open.

If you were an observer, this was a strange place to be getting it on. They were surrounded by mud, they couldn't quite lay down on the cold earth, but regardless of the scenery. Both farmer and clerk threw their clothes off, like they had ants in their pants. There was a small hesitant on Rakes part, when he saw Ruth take her bra off. She wasn't no child anymore, they were perfect, they for sure kicked the shit out of October's tits any day. Same thing happened to Ruth when Rake was at a full salute, she of course wasn't a virgin, but this would feel like the first time all over again.

The blue jeans were at the ankles of Rake, while Ruth just kicked her pants all the way off. she wasn't wearing any panties. Having sex because you were horny was great, but doing the nasty while having each other's hearts in hand, was amazing. Rake wrapped his tree trunk arms around the body of the gorgeous female.

Never in this life, would he have thought he was going to make love with this maiden. It was quite seriously like one of those pornos he watched. The young retail clerk comes and seeks out the pissed off farmer out in the corn field. She finds out that he's hungry and gives him something to eat, something that she cooked up herself, but now she's really feeding him with her body.

"I don't think we shou-

"Shut up Rake." Said Ruth, she had mounted him like frontal piggy back ride. "Just shut up and make love to me."

It didn't take much more than that to get him to comply. It was in and he was doing work on her, while she was hanging there with her arms around him, doing the same on her part. There were rapid thrusts and slow movements that made both of them feel like they finally feel alive. This is what sex felt like. This is how it felt to be wanted.

Rake felt horrible for doing this sin to his best friend's daughter, she was like a child with his age, but it was all legal, and she wanted it. He needed it; for Christ sake. She had one of the most amazing bodies he's seen in his lifetime. Even the naked girls he had underneath the bathroom sink were shit compared to Ruth.

"Rake?" She let escape her lips. Other sounds came too, only they seemed so easy to make while she felt all of Rake inside of her. It was like a branch, it hurt, but the pleasure drowned it out.

"Yes?" He was having the same trouble.

"I love you."

Rake hesitated for a second, just stanking there between Ruth's legs.

"I think I love you too."

"Do you think? Or do you know?"

Rake told her the truth. It felt almost felt better telling her, then fucking her.

"I do love you. I really do."

CHAPTER 15

WHILE OCTOBER LAID FLAT on her back of her own porch, and Rake was busy pounding Ruth's lady parts. Fred even had a knock on his door, but couldn't hear it because he was too busy smoking another cigarette, and reading the daily newspaper. Richard was having a war with himself if he should actually be a father from now on, or should he continue the drinking streak. It was because of him that Swers stayed in business.

All that was happening, while John sat in his chair and reviewed tape, after tape, after tape, until he thought he was watching the same movie over and over again. In a way he was, only the date and time was changing.

He sat there with his thumb in his mouth, chewing on the end, while the other hand went from the Play button; to the Fast Forward button. John couldn't help himself but to obsess over the book that; that reader promised to bring back in two days now. Henry said to try to keep busy and see if he could find out where his niece had run off to. It's been a little over a month now, and she was still missing.

Yes, he did kind of force his way of thinking on to his niece. Read a book each week, and you can have everything you ever dreamed of. Learn to be a cook and you'll become a cook. Learn to be a doctor and you'll become a doctor. Learn to save some money, and you'll become an investor.

Only the words of an adult, go in one ear and out the other. Especially when the kid is not wholly yours. Still John would pick a book and make her read it. He would do a pop quiz every now and again, and if she were to get the answer wrong. He would make her do inventory, which would take almost a year for one shelf.

There were nights that he would curse his sister for being so stupid for letting her legs be so drawn to the East and the West. Who was the father? His sister's guess was as good as his. Was good as the odds of winning the lottery. But that was wrong to think about. John wasn't that cold hearted person, even on his worse day. He just sometimes found his thoughts were going in boiling water, then fished them out before they become so severely burned.

All John knew was that if you're not ready for children, don't be going out having sex without protection. He knew it, because he read so many stories about the way women lives were shaped around such, unexpected pregnancies. If woman would actually pick up a fucking book every once in awhile, and get their noses out their phones, they would be vey educated woman that did have to grow up at the age of sixteen.

Yes there is a ton of women that read, but the ones that don't, out-weigh the ones that do, not a contest.

John then started thinking about the books he finished in one sitting, how they were so amazing, so able to hit him in all the right places, and that they had their own shelf, but at the same time were moved every week or so, to the shelf of life changing. It was that one shelf that was empty, then full, then empty, then full. Just like the way he was about reading. He could never get enough. But these thoughts were soon interrupted by his butler Henry.

"Sir, have you found the tape that Sopia is on yet?" Henry was taking a break from his duties, which were today, to make brunch, clean the dog; Horac, and make sure he was finding the book: Dr. Sleep on the internet. But had no such luck.

"I haven't seen her on these tapes yet. Are you sure you gave me the right dates?"

"Yes of course." Henry shuffled in his stance, wondering why his master ever doubts him so often. "Those are every angle in the building, are you sure you're watching the right camera angle?"

"Hen, I swear if you ask me again I'm gonna-"

Then just there down the hall from John's bedroom, was the girl. She crept down the hall ever so cunningly and quietly, that it took her almost an hour to be out of ear reach from her uncle's quarters. John even had to fast forward the damn television a smidge.

When she got close to Horac's quarters, she froze. The dog was no match for her without his wheels attached to him. But since he was missing the back legs, Horac started a whine that could be heard throughout the whole house. Good thing he slept like the wheels that were leaned up against the wall to the right of the his sleeping basket.

The Broken Pane

"If she would've only woken up that damn dog." Said John, his thumb was a slobbery red mess now.

"She is so brave and careful." Said Henry. He of course was the one that was always in awe at how fast a child can grow. "You can always tell when the kids are thinking. The little girl isn't a little girl anymore, when she is planning and pulling of escape plans right under our noses. I mean it took only twenty minutes to make it past my headquarters."

John wave his hand in the air, and told his Henry to hush.

He watched as she finally was in the clear, and started to run. She did all this with only a small piece of luggage. Only thing that John knew was that there was no book packed away in that case. He made sure of that. The books he made her read, were untouched in her room. Even the inventory showed that she didn't trouble herself one bit, to read even one word off the page of anything.

It took only a few minutes after that to see that she went through the Broken Pane to be one last smack to the face; John thought. She could've gone out a window on the first floor to avoid anymore kind of trouble, could've even broken a window by accident, but that would have been paid for.

"There she goes." Said John very sarcastically. "Not giving a shit about this family, and disrespecting the feelings of others."

"You mean to tell me you actually have feelings for Sophia?" Asked Henry. He was shocked that his tongue knew how to shape the word 'feelings'. "It wasn't your fault or hers, that she was put into this situation. You're just throwing a fit, because she didn't have the drive or passion to read, like you have the passion and drive to read."

John said nothing, because he knew this to be true. There was a reason he paid this man to be his servant. But moments like these, went way above his pay grade. Hen was like a big brother, or a wise teacher at times. He sometimes didn't put up with his shit, no matter how bad John threatened to fire him. It took only a few years to know that John couldn't survive without his dear old Hen

Sophia was gone now. Left in the middle of the night, and there was nothing he could do about it. He didn't call the police, they of course would "keep their eyes open", but didn't want to hear it from them. It would be easier to look and find a way to track her down *his* way, rather than leave it to someone that worked an eight hour shift.

He loved the girl, he truly did. But his love compared to the love of a mother, it was non-existing, but this was not his kid and her mother was not here to be her mother anyway. So he of course put out fliers around town, along with Hen, but people always seem to have their noses buried in their phones. It was the public's fault also, if they would just read something else for once, they might actually find her and call him.

"She'll be fine, sir." Said Henry. He placed his hand on the shoulder of his master. "There is not news that some twelve year old has been killed or be found, so I think that to be a sign that she is fine."

"I hope so Hen." John never took his eye off the open door of the Broken Pane.

*****

October's corpse stayed in a constant state of terror across the porch. The excess fluids and shit were about to be let out of her body, because when you're dead, it can't hold anything by itself anymore. October's life was thrown back into her body, like a pitcher would throw a ball 94 miles an hour.

She was back. What just happened? But she knew the truth. October had signed the contract the devil had conjured up. She saw the *thing*, the one that carried the wheel-barrow with all the dead bodies, with all the collected souls. Saw how it had been caressed, and that it showed no emotion only that it would never fail its mission.

Not even once.

There was another form of the boogeyman out in the world, one that hid in the dark shadows in alley ways, and behind the doors that swung open from bars. The monster that once lived in under the beds and in the closets, evolved into the best hide and seeker in existence.

October thought of this for a moment, she would have gotten up, but there was a sharp pain in her lower back and on the top of both her knuckles. But surprisingly, the sooner she noticed she had pain, the sooner it went away. Leaving her satisfied, like she hadn't orgasmed in over fifty years. As she layed there holding her head, she could feel the organs and bones, and tissue moving around in her own skin sack. People forget that we got all the proper bodily functions working, and that one major hiccup could send a person packing to the cemetery.

Her tits went up and firmed up, it sort of hurt, because she had been used to gravity taking control of them. Color seemed to be going back into her hair and skin, shoving all the imperfections out along with it. Like flakes of black ash, they fell all around her and blew away with the smallest of breeze.

It was a miracle.

Could the devil even be capable of such things? October thought she didn't think so. That old lumberjack had have been in heaven in order to make miracles happen. He was about the same as Santa Claus when it came to miracles, something that was built on a lie, but gave you something that you may or may not throw away.

Finally October had the strength and natural energy to stand right up and brush herself off. Even the pigment in her eyes was better, the green leaves was so green she could practically smell it, and the water from the water box, was throwing small gems here and there, as it fountained up and over.

It was absolutely amazing that she could focus without straining her eyes. Her back was straight and she felt taller, even athletic.

The book was closed at her feet. There was fresh blood on it, but this was from the old October, because the new one was healed and perfect. Perfect only if she collected souls that is, that was the deal she had made.

The book and her went inside the house, not even paying attention to the black scorch marks on the house, and that there was a crack that made it possible to see inside the living room. There was a scream caused by some wind, passing through the crack in the house, October paid no mind to this either. She needed a mirror that could help tell the truth, better than she was contemplating about what was actually happening. Seeing was believing, that was the truth one hundred percent.

When she looked in the bathroom mirror. It was like an old friend staring back at her, one that she wished she could give advice to, and make the wrongs in her life right. Or possibly have any man that turned to look at her.

The younger self of October looked back at her in denial. Thirty years shaved off like the hairs off her legs., and all that was left was her smooth skin. Her reflection stared back with eyes that she thought she would never see again. Ones that saw the world in 1080p again, instead of the all the white noise that moved around like some bad snow storm.

Her tears were like stones being dropped into a deep lake. Ones of happiness, an unknown emotion as of late. She hugged herself and stared a hole in the wall. It was wonderful. *Yes*, was the thought she had bouncing in her head. All the *no's* in life she received was finally met with one yes, and that made all the difference.

Reality of her being the way she was now, hadn't caught up yet. But when it did, she felt that the mirror might be dirty and it needed to be wiped with a firm hand. She need to be cleaned also, her robe was covered in black and red dust, red that could have been her blood. But this mirror needed cleaning.

When she got the cleaner from under the sink. There were some pictures of some naked eighteen year olds, with tits that were at least 36F, breast enhancements for sure she thought. October's thought for a moment that she was nothing compared the blonde slut, but recent events proved otherwise.

"You dumb fucking slut!"

With the force of a monkey thawing poop, she slammed her fist and the picture into the mirror, making a crashing sound, one that would get the dogs barking.

But they didn't.

October laughed for only a second, when she felt a sharp pain in her palm. A very deep slash, that looked like a red smile, opened up the skin. But it wasn't the accident alone that caught her laugh in her throat. It was the sight of her blood, that made her face look like nothing but a pair of eyes and a mouth.

A swarm of little red apples, the size of pennies, had fallen all over the floor and in the sink. They screamed and waved their stick arms and legs as they were shocked to see the world, almost as a new born baby would cry at the first bright light.

Their eyes were wide, and the tiny scream was so piercing that the rest of the glass that hung on the wall, fell into the sink and on the floor all around October. The scurried out of the way, trying to climb their way back into the cut in her hand.

The foot stepped on some broken glass, causing October to fall straight into the empty tub, that made an ugly fleshy sound.

Still, October didn't pay any attention to the pain in her feet and back, it was going away as she stared at her hand in amazement. The little red things were helping each other back into the red hole, from where they once came from. Like a scene from the 'Titanic', where it was only woman and children only.

As soon as they were out, they were back in. and four of the little buggers were pulling the two sides of the cut back together. Making sure that it was sealed, and they need to be more careful not to let something like that happen ever again.

There was a sick crunch sound in her back. Her back must have been out of place, from the impact, and the little red apples must have fixed that too.

"Fuck me." Was all that she could get out. You don't see something like that every day. Then again, you don't have a book that can send you to Hell. Where you can make deals with the Devil, if you eat the souls of children you might just have immortality. What sort of power was he indicating? The little red apples was the answer to her question. But it also raised more questions, like, what else could she do besides bleed an apple tree?

This time there was a knock at the door.

CHAPTER 16

LITTLE MATTY MCLEAN WAS a follower of Christ. Have been, since he was born, because his parents were Christians of the Victoria Church. He was baptized when he was not even a year old, but now that he was eight; going on nine, it was written on his heart like the writing in tombstones.

His hand was raised every single time the teacher in Sunday school would be lecturing about the Lord's stories. He knew them by heart, and he was determined to let the whole world know, that he indeed loved Jesus Christ. He thought that the whole concept of one man loving the world so much, that he sacrificed himself, so that we may be accepted into heaven after death. It was a beautiful thing, that you are loved the moment you are born, and forgiven when you have done something bad – when you are truly sorry of course – and that he was taking the path less traveled.

His father was so proud of him. He would take him door to door, so that he could preach the good news to all. The Sabbath may be on a Sunday, but the lords work was on the days of the week. Today was Saturday, and he was going to take him to the Plymouth territory, so that he could practice reading from the bible, to his fellow brother and sisters.

It also was a great tactic in which Christians used, to make sure that the doors didn't get slammed in their faces. It still happened, but some neighborhoods grew a heart when there was a child involved.

Matty had such a charismatic way of speaking, that even thought they would kindly decline the offer to hear the good news, they would at least listen to him read.

"You ready son?" said Matty's father. He was pulling up to the Blu's farm. It looked a little bit on the glum side. Like it was a little neglected, especially the driveway. "This one should be an easy one for you, October should be home by the looks of it."

"How do you know?" Asked Matty.

"Because Rake Blue sells all the local corn to Big Shop in Victoria. Did you know that son? But, anyways; his wife's name is October. I've only met her once."

"Well lets go read to her."

"You got it."

The engine was turned off, and they escalated their way to the door.

If Matty's father hadn't had his nose buried in his bible – just so he could make sure that Matty didn't lose his composure – he would have seen the black square and blood that stained the porch. Also the crack in the house, that made it easy to see inside the place. The blood was starting to dry, but some of it was now stuck to the bottom of both the bible thumpers dress shoes.

"Do you want me to knock? Or would you like to do the honors son?"

Matty would have done it, no problem, only there was a problem. It was like the unwritten laws of the supernatural or some shit like that. But only animals, and cameras, and children; were able to see what adults never see. Their brains were clouded with logic and reality, and never really used their imagination anymore. But right there in the crack, Matty could see there were two pair of eyes. Two pearls that floated in a black mist, they looked right at him. Eyes that looked into his heart, and made the urine inside him stir, and stir, and stir.

"No problem son, I'll do it." And he did.

Not more than five seconds later, there was an answer at the door.

"Hello, we're just out and about talking to you and your neighbors about what you think of where the world we live in is headed to?"

It took October a moment to answer. She was fixated on the little eight year old boy, that stood there with his bible in front of him like a shield.

"I'm sorry, what was the question again?" Asked October.

"Wait . . . are you like a niece of the Blu family? I know that Rake doesn't have any kids, but you sure don't look like October. You resemble her, but doesn't family always resemble family?"

". . . Yeah . . . I'm their niece, but it just so happens that my name is October too. It sort of runs in my family, on October's side; of course."

"Interesting, but no matter. Matty are you ready to read to . . . ?"

But Matty's father stop his sentence in its tracks, to see that his son had pissed and half soiled himself. He didn't take his eyes away from the crack, but the eyes were gone. Only they were in the head of the woman that stood at the door, but had changed so they were inviting, instead of what they really were.

The Broken Pane

"Matthew? Are you alright?" Said his father, bent down on one knee. So he could snap his son out of his horrible day dream.

"I'm so sorry miss Blu, but I gotta go. I just, oh no . . . "

He scooped up Matty, and hurried him to the car. What had happened to his Matty?

He wouldn't have noticed that October had scurried just a little out of the house, to try and grab the little boy from the man's hands. She was hungry, so hungry; she had bit the inner gums inside her mouth, so she didn't actually bite the boy.

How long would she be able to hold the urge off? Did it matter? She needed to eat something, and the flesh of children was the only thing that can satisfy it.

She couldn't. If it hadn't been for the book that she gotten from John Silence, she wouldn't have seen what she's seen. Although it did make her young and sexy. Maybe a bit horny too, but that could wait. Rake had to come home sometime, and even though she looked like she just turned thirty, she's going to give the man what he wanted all these years.

But she had to make a difference. Maybe if she gave the book back to the rightful owners. It would all go away. She would be back to normal, and she could talk one last time with the man that she loved, and maybe make a difference. Yes, she thought that it would make things better.

Taking the book back to the Broken Pane would – in October's eyes – would make things all better. Like a customer returning some bad merchandise he recently purchased, so he could spend his money on something else. She was wrong, but denial was a strong drug, that always gets you when you least expect it.

*****

"That was fun. I didn't think I could last that long on a first go around." Said Rake. He and Ruth lay on the soft dirt that had a little sun, so it wouldn't be cold when they were through making love.

"Is that all you have to say about it? It was fun?" asked Ruth.

"Well honestly I don't know what to say. Maybe I shouldn't have said anything at all."

"That's not what I meant. I think you're just gorgeous, and I don't want you to change anything about you. I asked it, because I too thought it was fun."

"Well, just know that I'm still married, and what we did was wrong. But I can't help but think I did the right thing at the same time."

"I think I did the right thing too."

They were both naked, laying on top of their clothes. Something interesting struck Rake about the young store clerk. Is even though they were done making babies, she didn't hurry to get her tits covered. He couldn't help but compare her to his wife. October would have thought just taking her pants off, would be enough. But every guy knew that if she wasn't completely naked, it felt like a pity fuck.

"You're very beautiful. In all my life, I would never had thought you felt this way about me. I've watched you grow up. You've been through a tough time in your life."

Ruth didn't say anything for a bit. Her eyes made Rake's feelings at ease.

"I'm a big girl now, as you can see. I have been through a tough time, but I'm over it now. My dad isn't the same man he once was, which puts me into being the new mom for my sisters. But its going to be okay. They're not dead, they have nice things, and they have someone that shows them attention when its needed."

The old farmer held Ruth in his arms, and tightened his hold on her just a smidge. He took what she said in, and wanted to make sure he processed it well. He did, and kissed her on the head.

"I just worry. I haven't worried about anyone for a long time."

"Your wife couldn't have been that bad for you. I mean, you stayed with her all your life."

"It wasn't all bad, no. I think it was because I still had hope that we would someday have a baby, and all the doctors charts were all just lies. Then one year turned into two years, two turned into five. Now its been however long, and we just quietly decided not to try." Rake's hand was making a motion every time he talked. It made Ruth love him more. "There were a couple times I thought about shooting myself with my shotgun, I keep in my closet."

"Don't say that please. I'm here now, I may be just some young girl to you, but I'm a young girl with a brain that thinks, and actions that speak louder than words. I love you Rake. Please don't take yourself away from me. I have you now, and I don't know what I would do if I lost you."

Rake sat up, which made Ruth sit up with him. "I love you too! I really do, I've made my decision. Let's be together."

"You would have to go tell October how you really feel."

"For you, I would do it as soon as I can get my clothes on. I mean it."

She believed him, now that the dirt was dry, and falling off their bodies. They helped each other get up, and couldn't get their clothes on faster.

*****

Now that Henry calmed down his master. Gave him a classic book to read, *A Christmas Carol*, one that Mr. Silence has read only nineteen times. That sort of story was so well written; it stood the test of time. Henry knew it would keep him busy, knowing that he would read it twenty times, a small achievement in his master's eyes.

Henry could take this time to see if he could find a copy of Dr. Sleep anywhere. He could buy someone out, and have them deliver it straight away. But it wouldn't be here till the next day. That wouldn't do, that would only cause his master to turn a darker shade of blue. The color of stress.

A whole hour went by, as he sat there on his desktop, looking at countless sites that said 'SOLD OUT' written on the title of Dr. Sleep. It was tedious work. But, he loved his job and his master, so he drank a cup of coffee every three websites. Then took a small break to go get more.

It was then he saw a young woman opening the door that leads into the hallway to the house-side of the mansion. This time, Horac didn't have his wheels on; so he couldn't go say hello in his defensive bark like that one reader. *What was her name again?* I must have been some sort of month.

He made its way to the kitchen, where he would head off the female visitor.

"Hello there reader? May I be of any help to you?"

"Henry its me, I've come to return the book I borrowed from you guys yesterday. Its here in my pur-"

"Why do you have October's book?" Asked Henry. He was very concerned and confused.

The more October thought she was normal, the more she thought that she wasn't normal. This sort of thing doesn't happen, and she *was* beautiful. But she was unrecognizable.

"I'm October's niece, would you believe me if I told you my name is also October?" The lie worked on that bible thumper and his delicate cookie he called a son. "She told me where to find you, and where to go."

"Is that so? Well I think my master would love to see what you have for him. I apologize for cutting you off earlier. You said it was in your purse?"

"It is." She patted her bag.

"Right this way reader."

Henry knew that there was a difference between a wise old man, and a horny old man. He wasn't anywhere near being some old horn dog, but seeing October walk in front of him, was making tap into some cruel intentions he thought he never had. He thought of how he would just grab her by the back of the neck, and do it doggie style right there in the hallway. Henry just shook his head, and thought of what his master would say, to keep his mind off the skeleton in his closet.

"Sir, may I introduce miss October. The niece of that reader we had yesterday. She has something for you."

Before John Stood up, he turned on the rose bush camera, and the television in front of him came to life, showing the three members standing in the triangular shape.

"You're the niece of October? The one that borrowed the book? The book titled: The Boss?"

"I am, and I have it right here."

October swore on Jesus' pole, swore on all the dead ancestors that she never knew, and swore on the relationship she still had left with the man she loved. She swore she put the book inside of her purse. But it wasn't there.

"Where is it?" Asked John, his eyes twinkled with delight.

She looked at him in fright. He was a lot taller and broader than she remembered. October felt if she told him the truth, he would punch a hole in her chest.

"It was in here, I swear." Pleaded October.

"Hen? Is this some sort of joke?" John's teeth were clenched, and there looked like there was a tear falling down his face. Then he slumped down in his chair before anyone of them could answer.

"I'm so sorry Henry, John. I was telling the truth."

John just sat in his throne, with his head in his hand, looking at the screen with bitter taste. It took him awhile to notice it, but it was there, as clear as a sky without clouds. On the shoulder of woman, whose name was also October, was a creature. One claw was deep inside one ear, and the other one was sunken inside the white of her arm. It was black, and had the eyes that looked like pearls, ones that floated together in the dark waters of the ocean. They stared at Mr. Silence, then a smile formed that almost cut its own head off when it did. It's teeth were all like razor blades that would have clicked together, if the sound from the cameras picked it up.

John wasted no time.

He shot up like a dart, and came around the chair at October. His hands were the size of the hardback books he had been reading all these years. He reached out and slapped the female square in the face.

"Get the fuck out of my house! You witch!"

John's face was the color of red now. The color of pissed off.

Never in his life would he hit a woman, never, but this was no woman. This was a servant of Satan. Part of the servants that killed his father when he was in a deep sleep.

*****

When the two love birds, made their way to the truck, they held hands. This felt wonderful, it was up there with having sex in a cornfield.

"I gotta get home so I can change. I kinda got my clothes ruined." Said Ruth, leaning against her truck.

"I might have helped that along. I'm sorry."

"Don't be sorry, just don't make a habit of it. But there is a place on our clothes that helps get it off easier."

Rake laughed at that.

"Hey look over there." Said Rake. He pointed way across the fields of Plymouth. There was a house, a huge house at that, and there was some dust that was kicked up by someone. That was what caught his eye.

"I don't know. I've never found the time to see who else lived in these parts of the woods." She laughed too. Rake just made her so happy.

"That's interesting. We should go see it tonight, or something . . . "

"Are you saying that you might want to take me out on a date?" Ruth turned red, she almost jumped up in the air, but she kept herself.

It was like a light went on in Rake's head. "That's exactly what I'm trying to say. Would you wanna go with me? It doesn't have to be over there, it could be anywhere you want."

Ruth stayed quiet for awhile. She wanted to make him sweat it out for a little bit, he just looked like Tarzan trying to meet Jane for the first time. "Yes I would love to go with you. But only if you take care of your business, and spend the night with me tonight. Don't worry about my dad, I always get what I want."

That may be the whole truth. The broken man Ruth called her father, would do anything to make his daughters happy. She was smart to get everything out on the table right here and now, so everyone didn't go spreading rumors.

They could go spreading the truth.

"I will go home and tell my wife, that I want a divorce, and that I'm moving out."

"That's all I want you to do."

"When did you start being a woman?" Asked Rake, his hand was pushing back a strand of hair.

"When you started treating me like a woman." Ruth smiled and opened up her truck. She wanted to get the cool air blowing, so she needed to reach way in there.

When she did, there were hands on the waist of her jeans that pulled them down to her knees. Rake was ready for seconds, and Ruth was just surprised at this. But she let him, and she loved it. The thought of someone seeing them made her love it more and more. This was love, when you did the things you wanted to do, when you wanted to do them, not matter what happens in this world.

She was wrong, but you can't think about that stuff when you're reaching your climax for the second time in a row.

*****

As soon as she was in there, October got out. The impact on her face did hurt like a fuck! Only for a few moments though, the little red apples were moving around inside; trying to patch up the damage to their fleshy house.

She got in her car, shut the door, and before starting the engine; she looked into the mirror to see if the bruise was gone. It was, but is she hadn't ran away from the black man, John would have done far worse, October was sure of it.

Only now, October was different. She had to lie about her identity to strangers. The book *was* in her purse, but she didn't know what happened to it? Everything wasn't the way it was supposed to be anymore.

Only there was a hunger that she couldn't keep at bay. It was making her foam at the mouth, and was putting evil thoughts in her head. Then she raced off the property, leaving a billow of dust in her wake. The thoughts in her head were literally killing everything around her. The road seemed to get hot enough, to melt the tar that filled in the cracks.

The book and her were now one. The lumberjack; that was the second born of God, knew she would try to stop what they had agreed on. So he magically put the book back into the place she would easily find it again.

A sign said 'SPEED LIMIT 40', but she was flying down the road towards home at even 75, if she was going just five miles over the meter, she would have missed Rakes truck. The truck that she used to ride in next to him all those years ago. But now there was another vehicle, and a girl bent over it, and October's husband was on the end of that girl.

Little red apples were bleeding out of the lips of October. They fell in her lap, and rubbed their head on impact, then started climbing the clothes so they could get back home.

She would've stopped. She should've stopped. But that would have caused her to crash into the fields, draw attention to herself, maybe even make her explode if she was hit in the right way. Then what? The little red apples just get up and start building her back to normal? October didn't want to find out.

Instead she was home now. In less than twenty minutes – felt like five – and came to find out that there was some little girl on the front porch. From the looks of it, she had something behind her back. She just stood there, and waited to see what

October would do to her now that she was caught.

"Who are you?" Asked October, in a firm voice. She was out of her car, and was already upon the little girl, to see what answer she had for her.

"I was just hungry. I didn't mean to, I never would have gone this far if I wasn't desperate enough, please don't call the police on me." The girl pleaded. There was a gift card from Big Shop in her hand. That must have been what was hiding behind her back. Trying to pick the lock with a card, that was so old school.

"Well I'm not going to call the police on you. Its very rude to come home and find a complete stranger trying to break into your house, I have important things in there. Wait a minute." October looked the girl up and down for a few seconds. "You're that girl that I met at Big Shop, what did you say your name is again?"

It took her a few minutes to recollect. "Yes, I remember, your name is October right? I'm Sophia, I'm the one that told you about the old book hop. Did you go?"

October's eyes got wide with realization. "No I didn't. Hungry did you say? So am I, would you like to come inside?"

She pushed past Sophia, and threw the key into the lock. The door was left open, so the little girl could come in behind her. October hoped she did, because for a moment she felt a shudder of relief, as she saw the white book sitting on kitchen counter.

Sophia did. Shutting the door, and taking a seat on the love seat. "October, there is a broken picture in here."

"There is?" October came into the living room and picked up the photo, making sure she didn't cut herself on the glass. "I never noticed it, but . . . thank you."

It was strange thing to say, but what do you say in a situation like this? It was a wedding picture of Rake and her, but that was when they were actually happy.

Then it hit October, Sophia didn't seem to notice that October was any younger or out of place. It must be that small power working in her favor. Or working in her bosses favor, is that why the book is named The Boss?

"Would you like to watch The Wizard of Oz? Its one of my favorites." She didn't even wait for Sophia's response, and clicked the clicker, then the movie was playing. Dorthy and the Scarecrow, was talking to the enchanted trees about what apples are good, and what apples are bad.

"I'll just go fix you something in the kitchen, and bring it out to you. Would you like that?"

"Yes please. You know, I just knew you were a nice person the moment I first met you. That's why I told you about the book hop in the first place, my uncle always told me that; its the readers that are the best people to talk to."

October patted the twelve year olds head and disappeared into the kitchen.

*****

Sophia watched as Dorthy and Scarecrow found the Tin Woodsman, and started to oil up his joints. She too also loved this movie, it was an instant classic, one that her grand-kids would remember forever and ever, if she had any. Some handsome boy one day would ask her to marry him, and if she loved him enough, she would indeed say "yes".

The Tin-mans song was next, *If I Only Had A Heart,* that was her favorite of all time. She started singing along with it in her head, and was about to wonder what October was going to bring her.

That was when she got her answer. There was the sound of ringing and she began to become dizzy. Then there was another sound of ringing, except if was a much louder ringing, and her vision turned to a veil of red. Her body just fell down to the floor, and she was on her back. Looking up at the ceiling, it was starting to grow black strands of hair, and it fell all around her.

The floor below her started to move up and down, and her legs started to get tight together, then they seemed to be crushed. Then it was her knees, and then her thighs.

She couldn't cry out, because the impact done on her brain must have damaged that part. All she could do is hear, feel, and see. It was her waist that exploded beneath her, and the part of the song; . . . *if I only had a heart* . . . , then before her head was swollen up and crushed. Sophia could see the giant body of a demon, one that was grey, and that was chocking on her body as it ate her. Like a bird would try to swallow its food whole. Then it was darkness.

*****

Just like when she could feel her body changing when she was sprawled out on the front porch. October could feel her body change, only it was more horrific, then it was a benefit. Her hair grew out thick and quick, knocking things over and falling into other rooms of the house. Even her size grew, giving her more teeth and a bigger stomach lined with teeth. October could feel every single one of them.

Some sort of horn, pushed its way out of every part of her body. Her head, her face, her elbows, even the fingers she wore, were replaced with some sort of hooks.

The transformation was like a sexual pleasure to October, because she was finally going to do her part of the contract, and finally eat something. The old October no longer was present, and the new one quietly protruded into the other room, and smashed the young girl across the head.

It made popping sound that might have punctured a hole into her skull. Then she hit her again for good luck, causing her to fall to the floor. Then she began to eat.

When she was done. Like magic, she slowly became her thirty year old self again. Only she had the belly of a nine month pregnant woman. She held herself, like a mother would do when she felt her baby move for the first time inside of her.

This made October smile. She always wanted to have a child inside of her, and now she did. Smiling like some maniac that might know something you don't know, but you would soon find out.

Then there was a huge laugh that came from her mouth. The evilest cackle a follower of the devil could get out. It rang through the town of Plymouth.

END OF PART 1